The Secret Zoo: Raids and Rescues
Copyright © 2013 by Bryan Chick

The text of this book is set in 10 1/2-point Arrus BT.
Book design by Paul Zakris

Library of Congress Cataloging-in-Publication Data

Chick, Bryan.
Raids and rescues / Bryan Chick.
pages cm—(The Secret Zoo ; [5])
"Greenwillow Books."
Summary: Noah, Megan, Richie, and Ella must navigate a maze of never-ending aquariums in the Secret Zoo to rescue their animal friends.
ISBN 978-0-06-219228-8 (trade edition)
[1. Zoos—Fiction. 2. Zoo animals—Fiction.
3. Secret societies—Fiction. 4. Human-animal relationships—Fiction.
5. Rescues—Fiction. 6. Friendship—Fiction.] I. Title.
PZ7.C4336Rai 2013 [Fic]—dc23 2013008584

13 14 15 16 CG/RRDH 10 9 8 7 6 5 4 3 2 1
First Edition

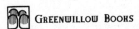
GREENWILLOW BOOKS

THE SECRET ZOO

RAIDS AND RESCUES

BRYAN CHICK

GREENWILLOW BOOKS
An Imprint of HarperCollinsPublishers

FOR THE STUDENTS AND TEACHERS
AT NORTH SASHABAW ELEMENTARY.
YOU GUYS ROCK!

PRELUDE

THE CAPTIVES

DeGraff, the Shadowist, backed away from the portal to the City of Species, something of a smile on what remained of his face. He turned and moved deeper into the Creepy Critters sector of the Secret Zoo, the thing-that-had-once-been-a-bear walking beside him. Seconds ago, the animal had delivered a note to Mr. Darby—a note with a very simple message: *I'm back, old friend.*

As DeGraff moved through the long corridor, he gazed at aquariums set in the walls. Most were cracked and chipped and covered in mold and moss, their once-captive inhabitants free to roam the building.

Cocoons and stringy moss dangled from a high ceiling.

Bugs and lizards covered the walls, the floor, the ceiling. Plump-bodied spiders crawled along the aquariums, millipedes squirmed through gaping cracks in the glass, and scorpions scurried about. Snails dragged themselves along, trails of slime marking their paths. Winged bugs flew in circles, bouncing off one another. As DeGraff walked, he stepped though cobwebs and his boots crunched down on the hard shells of beetles and other unnameable things.

Thinking of the traps set throughout the halls, the corners of his mouth curled with another attempt at a smile. He was ready for them to come. He'd had a year to prepare.

At the entrance of a branching corridor, a door stood coated in bugs. In the outside world, a similar corridor in Creepy Critters was called Bugs-A-Bunch, but DeGraff rarely thought of it by name here. He gripped the handle and a few slow-to-move slugs burst beneath his fingers. Flinging the door open, he stepped inside, the mangy thing-that-had-once-been-a-bear following.

In this corridor, the dirt walls between the aquariums resembled those of a cave. A few flickering torches provided the only light. Hordes of snakelike insects squirmed along the hard floor, occasionally dropping down into the dirty fur of the bear—or the thing which had once been one.

As DeGraff passed a torch, his shadow was cast onto the wall. The dark spot lost its form and took a shape independent of his own. It skimmed the walls, churning the loose dirt and knocking down insects like the slow sweep of a broom.

When DeGraff reached the end of an aisle lined with fish-filled aquariums, he stepped into the Creepy Core, a large, circular room capped with a high, concrete dome. The air stank of mildew, mold, and decay. In the middle of the room stood a man. His hair and eyebrows were bright red, and his face was splotchy with freckles: Charlie Red, once a security guard from the Clarksville Zoo.

In the ground behind Charlie was a deep pit closed off with glass. Four people were far below, Tank and three teenage Descenders, Secret Cityzens who had just been captured by the Shadowist. They were still unconscious, lying on the dirt floor with their arms and legs stretched out. Hannah's long, red-dyed bangs covered her face like a mask, and a few bugs were crawling over her bare feet. The fair skin of Sam's cheeks was bloodied, and Tameron's and Tank's dark skin was streaked with mud.

At Charlie's feet lay a bundle of clothes and equipment—jackets, boots, a hat, a backpack. It was the gear that gave the Descenders their magical strength.

"We got 'em," Charlie said.

DeGraff kept quiet. A small swarm of mosquitoes

landed on his face, fed on the poison of his blood, and dropped lifelessly to the ground. He scanned the captives in the pit, then kicked softly through their belongings at Charlie's feet. The thing-that-had-once-been-a-bear sniffed the canvas backpack.

"Not all of them," he answered at last. His rumbly, wet-sounding voice seemed to come from a part of his body that was barely working. "Are the portals closed?"

Charlie nodded. "All but the main entrance into the City of Species."

"Excellent." DeGraff smiled his vile smile. "Darby and his minions—they'll be coming soon. The message has been delivered." The Shadowist wrung his hands together, spreading sticky snail guts across his leather gloves. "Keep watch on the prisoners, Mr. Red. I'll check on our team."

"Yes, sir," Charlie said.

The Shadowist turned and touched the mangy, broad head of the thing-that-had-once-been-a-bear. "Come," he said. "Let's go find your friends."

CHAPTER 1

In The News Again

"You kids ready to go?" Mrs. Nowicki called from the upstairs bathroom in Noah's house. "I don't want to be late for school again today."

"Just about!" Noah said. Then he waved his sister, Megan, and their friends Ella and Richie into the dining room, where the family laptop was sitting on the table. He pulled up a chair and opened an internet browser as his friends leaned in around him. Then he clicked on a link to a national news site hosting the story of the two escaped zoo animals that had destroyed parts of Clarksville Elementary.

"Turn it up," Megan said as the video began to play.

Noah did, but just loud enough so that the four friends had to lean toward the speakers to hear. A news reporter began to describe "another bizarre event in the quiet community of Clarksville, the same city where, a year ago, a young girl named Megan Nowicki spent three weeks trapped in the cellar of a museum." News footage showed scenes of Clarksville: the historic clock tower, the neighborhood streets, the zoo. As the video switched to the damaged grounds of Clarksville Elementary, the reporter's tone became very serious as he described what had happened three days ago, on Halloween night.

"As Clarksville children were trick-or-treating, two animals—a polar bear and a rhinoceros—somehow managed to escape the city zoo and wander onto the grounds of the nearby school. There they destroyed several pieces of playground equipment before ultimately smashing their way inside, where they caused thousands of dollars in damage to school property before finally being contained by police and Animal Control officers."

The video footage switched to a large crowd of protestors outside a building in downtown Clarksville. People were pacing and waving picket signs.

The reporter's story continued: "When news spread that the two beloved zoo animals were scheduled for euthanization, there was an immediate outcry. Crowds of protesters gathered at the Animal Control office. Most called for the animals to be returned to the wild. But officials saw a problem with this."

The video footage switched to a bald man with a bushy mustache. He stated that animals raised in controlled environments rarely adapt well to their natural habitats.

The video then switched back to the crowd of protesters, and the reporter said, "Several animal rights groups converged on the city of Clarksville, demanding the animals' release."

The camera switched to a bearded man with a jagged scar on his cheek. He was waving a sign and passing out flyers with the heading, "Free them or we will!" Every time a reporter asked his name, the man shook his head and bumped the reporter's microphone away.

The reporter went on. "Just yesterday, a decision was made to transfer the two animals to the Waterford Zoo, just west of Clarksville. This neighboring zoo contains more traditional exhibits—caged enclosures which make escape virtually impossible. The animals are scheduled for transfer soon."

As the video ended, Noah said, "What do you think?"

Ella shrugged. "It's nothing we don't already know. I mean—it's not like that story hasn't been on the news something like twenty-three hours a day."

"You didn't notice him?"

"Notice who?"

Noah stared over the top of the computer monitor to make sure his mom was still upstairs. Then he rewound to a previous scene showing the bearded man with the scar standing among a crowd of protestors. He hoisted a sign in the air that read, "Free them or we will!"

Noah glanced at his friends, his eyes wide.

"Yeah . . ." Ella said. "Goofy-looking dude with a big sign—so what?"

"He doesn't look familiar?"

The scouts stared harder.

"The Secret Zoo," Noah said. "He's a Crosser—one of the Constructors that helped repair the aquariums in Creepy Critters on the night the sasquatches tried to escape."

Ella's and Megan's expressions changed.

"You're right!" Megan said.

"Sooo . . . he's also an animal activist?" Ella asked.

Noah shook his head. "He's just pretending to be."

"Why?"

Noah clicked a mouse button to close out the video. "Because Blizzard and Little Bighorn are going home." He smiled at his friends and added, "The Secret Society . . . they're going to break them out."

At school recess a few hours later, the scouts rushed out onto the playground, much of which was still roped off for repairs from damage the world believed had been done by an escaped polar bear and rhinoceros, but which the scouts knew had been committed by monstrous creatures known as sasquatches. The first days of November had brought unseasonably cold weather and a dusting of snow. Now, a few snowflakes fell from a gray sky to rest in wood chips and stick to steel bars. The scouts wore their usual headgear: Richie, the cotton cap with the large pom-pom; Ella, her fluffy pink earmuffs; Megan, her sporty fleece headband; and Noah, the red hunting cap he'd discovered in the Secret Zoo.

They huddled close to discuss the video and take guesses at what Mr. Darby and the Secret Council were planning. Minutes into their conversation, a blue spot streaked through the air and touched down on Noah's shoulder: Marlo, a malachite kingfisher barely bigger than Noah's thumb. In his bill was a neatly folded slip of paper. An Instant Marlo.

"Hey, buddy," Noah said.

Marlo chirped a hello as Noah opened the message and quietly read it.

My Dear Scouts,

I regret it has taken so long to deliver a message. Things have been busy. I would like to invite the four of you

to an emergency session of Council. Can you meet me
at Chickadee Lane tomorrow after school? Please send
your reply with Marlo, and plan on being away no
more than two hours.

Best wishes,
Mr. Darby

"Guys—what do you think?" Noah asked. "We clear for tomorrow?"

Everyone nodded. Richie plucked a pen from his shirt pocket and handed it to Noah, who scribbled down a response, folded the note, and handed it back to Marlo. The kingfisher jumped off his shoulder and flew out of sight.

CHAPTER 2

THE COLD CLOSET

Noah spent the better part of the evening in his bedroom trying to finish an English paper. Instead of working, he mostly sat back in his chair, tapping his pencil in his lap and staring off into space. He kept seeing DeGraff, three days ago, in the old dirt cellar beneath his school, the way he'd taken down the Descenders and dragged them off, their bodies passing in and out of the shadows. Where were the captives now? Were they injured? Alive? Every time Noah imagined the lifeless bodies of his friends, he tried to push his thoughts aside.

Around eight o'clock, someone rang the porch bell. From

outside came a familiar, hoarse voice—Mr. Connolly, their neighbor from across the street. Mr. Connolly was not coping well with his recent divorce. He stopped by every few days, and Noah's parents always invited him in for a snack. Tonight proved to be no exception, and before long Noah heard his mother say, "Come in, Peter, please" and then the rattle of silverware.

"How are you?" Mrs. Nowicki asked.

"Oh . . . good, good." It was a lie, of course. If Mr. Connolly were good, he wouldn't be standing in Noah's living room again.

"Cookie?"

"I shouldn't—"

"Butter pecan."

"Well . . . maybe, sure."

A kitchen chair rumbled as it pulled across the floor, and that meant there would be two fewer cookies for Megan and Noah this week. Noah would have resented this if the person downstairs were anyone but Mr. Connolly, a kind old man who didn't deserve to be alone.

At ten o'clock, Noah's parents walked Mr. Connolly out and then headed up to Noah's room to wish him good night. Once they'd gone, Noah opened his second-story window, stuck his head out into the cold, and stared at Fort Scout, his old tree house. Inside it, Noah knew, a Descender and at least one zoo animal were posted, keeping a watchful eye over the east wall of the Clarksville Zoo.

Noah ducked back inside and slid the window closed. Time to get ready for bed.

His closet was a small walk-in, perhaps six feet deep and across. He gently tugged a chain to turn on the overhead light and scanned the messy stack of clothes for something to sleep in. Standing there, he suddenly realized how chilly the closet was. His carpeted floor felt more like cold concrete.

He squatted in front of the heat vent and felt warm air blowing out. The furnace was working fine.

"Weird . . ." he muttered.

He snatched a pair of sweatpants and a T-shirt off the shelf and headed out of the closet, tugging the chain on his way. In bed, he tucked the covers up to his chin and quickly warmed up.

❧ CHAPTER 3 ❧

CHICKADEE LANE AND
THE KIDDIE TRAIN

When their class was dismissed on Wednesday afternoon, the scouts snatched their jackets from their lockers and headed outdoors. They hurried across the school grounds, crossed Jenkins Street, then ran through the west gates of the Clarksville Zoo. Within minutes, they reached Chickadee Lane.

Two small buildings were joined by a winding breezeway with open walls. Chickadees flew freely in and out, pecking at feeders and raining seeds down their white-feathered breasts.

"There he is," Richie said. He pointed to where

Mr. Darby stood, feeding a chickadee that had perched in his open palm. His long gray hair was pulled back in a ponytail, and his bushy beard lay across his chest.

The scouts followed a pathway of colorful brick pavers that wound through a crowded garden. Feeders and nesting boxes dangled from the limbs of bushes and the eaves of a gabled rooftop.

Mr. Darby turned to the scouts and smiled. Even on the gray, overcast day, he wore his sunglasses. But he'd traded his customary velvet jacket for a simpler jacket. He looked oddly ordinary this way, like someone's grandfather rather than the leader of a secret kingdom filled with animals and magic.

"Probably not a good idea for me to get caught with a chickadee in my hand," the old man said. He lightly tossed the bird into the air, where it darted out of sight. "But one can hardly resist the temptation."

"To hold the animals?" Megan asked.

"No," he answered. "To be so loved."

The scouts stayed quiet until Ella broke the silence. "Okay . . . what's the status, Mr. D?"

Mr. Darby peered in all directions to make certain no one was around. Then he leaned toward the scouts and in a hushed voice said, "We're doing what we promised ourselves we'd never do—jeopardize the secrecy of the Secret Zoo to rescue some of our own." He paused and adjusted his sunglasses. "Blizzard and Little Bighorn—we're going after them."

"We know," Noah said.

Mr. Darby pulled back his shoulders and stood very straight. "You *know*?"

Ella said, "We happened to watch an animal activist in town for a visit. He looked a lot like a Secret Cityzen we once met."

Mr. Darby considered this. "I sometimes forget how curious and perceptive the four of you are." A chickadee jumped out of the bushes and landed on the old man's shoulder. Mr. Darby politely brushed it off, then turned and headed down the breezeway, saying, "Let's find a spot protected from curious eyes, yes?"

The scouts followed him down the brick path and stepped into one of the small buildings. Mr. Darby waited to speak until the door fell closed behind them.

"If Blizzard and Little Bighorn disappear from the Waterford Zoo, there certainly needs to be a good reason. Our Constructor—our fake protestor—will provide that reason. We hope people will believe that a fictitious, unnamed group of animal activists abducted our animals."

Richie said, "And you think people will actually buy that?"

"They will when they see the signs."

"What signs?"

"The flyers that our Crosser has been distributing will be scattered throughout the Waterford Zoo."

Megan asked, "But don't you think people will freak out when no one can find two missing zoo animals?"

As the old man shrugged, a chickadee perched on his shoulder. He softly stroked the bird's head with one finger and said, "Hello, Chubs." It still amazed Noah to think that Mr. Darby knew all the animals' names.

Mr. Darby said, "I've decided that's not my concern. I once believed I could offer up Blizzard and Little Bighorn as sacrifices to protect our world, but I've since learned that I can't. My only ambition now is to rescue my beloved Gifteds and bring them home."

"What about Tank and the Descenders?" Noah asked. "How do we rescue them?"

"The Secret Council is convening right now to take a look at some information we've gathered. And we'd like you to join us. Noah's been closer to DeGraff than anyone in our recent history—he might have valuable insight. Plus we have something else to discuss with you—to *propose* to you, actually."

"Oh boy," Richie said.

A second chickadee touched down on Mr. Darby's shoulder. The old man raised his hand and allowed it to jump to his index finger.

"Why, hello there—" His sentence stopped short. He drew the bird away from his eyes and then pulled it back a few inches again, as if trying to bring it into focus. "Why . . . what's your name, little one? I can't seem to . . ." He moved the bird forward and back again.

"Looks like it's time to give up fashion for function and trade in those sunglasses for some bifocals," Ella teased.

Mr. Darby flicked his wrist and tossed away the chickadee, which struggled to get its wings in rhythm. "Yes, well . . ." He gently swiped the other chickadee off his shoulder and said somewhat urgently, "Let's go, shall we?" He brushed past the scouts and pulled open the door. When he stepped outside, snow swirled around his feet. He began to walk off, the scouts following.

"I know our time is limited," Mr. Darby went on. "So I've arranged for a ride back to Giraffic Jam, which has an easy portal to the Secret Zoo."

"A ride?" Richie asked.

Mr. Darby swept his arm toward a nearby building with open walls and a wooden floor—a railway platform to board the Clarksville Zoo train, which stood waiting there.

"Care to go aboard?"

The old man walked to the rear of the train and climbed on. The scouts piled in, Richie beside Mr. Darby, the other scouts in the seat across from them. Ella, sitting directly in front of Richie, kept banging her knees against his as the two jostled for space.

"*C'mon!*" Ella said. "Give me some room, would you?"

"I can't!" Richie complained as he shifted his rear end to find new places for his legs. "Not without sitting on the roof!"

"Sounds good to me," Ella quipped. "Or maybe you could go lie on the tracks."

Mr. Darby smiled his patient smile, then turned and waved his hand toward the front of the train. The engineer gave a thumbs-up out the window, and seconds later the engine rumbled to life. The train jolted forward and back as old rods and rusty cranks began to turn the wheels. Megan's glasses jumped to the tip of her nose, and the pom-pom on Richie's cap wobbled.

Noah watched puffs of steam spout into the air from the engine's chimney.

"Mr. Darby?" Noah said.

"Yes?" the old man said as he gazed at the passing zoo. A bright yellow finch flew through an open window and landed on his arm. It tipped its head and tweeted.

The world suddenly turned black as the train plunged into a tunnel. Noises blurred into a single sound, and slivers of light streamed by from cracks in the concrete walls. Everyone stayed quiet. After almost a minute, the train shot back out into the open and then followed a long curve in the track to rumble into Arctic Town. Noah stared out toward the Polar Pool and wondered about Blizzard, how badly he was hurt and if he was afraid.

"What about Charlie Red?" Noah asked. "I mean . . . I can't believe he turned on us!"

A heavy frown formed on Mr. Darby's suddenly stern face. "A shocking betrayal, yes."

"How long has he been with DeGraff?"

The old man began to stroke his long gray beard. "Who can know?"

"Do we even know how long DeGraff's been in the Secret Zoo?"

"Many months, I'm certain. Especially if we consider what he was able to do with our magic."

Noah knew exactly what he was referring to—DeGraff's portal to Clarksville Elementary.

"It no doubt took DeGraff some time to figure out how to portal beyond the boundaries of the Clarksville Zoo," Mr. Darby said. "The Secret Society has never been able to accomplish this."

Megan, suddenly a bit pale, leaned over her knees. "Do you think DeGraff's been able to build other tunnels? Portals to new spots?"

Mr. Darby shrugged. "The prospect, quite frankly, is horrifying."

Noah wondered about this. Where would DeGraff

go? How *far* could he go? Beyond Noah's neighborhood? Outside the country? And what could he do with his magic in these places?

"Horrifying . . ." Mr. Darby repeated.

Noah said, "The curtain—the one from the school— did Solana give it to you?"

Mr. Darby nodded. "She did. And our magical scientists are hard at work studying it. I assure you they have not rested since the curtain was delivered to them."

A second finch found a spot on Mr. Darby's shoulder. This one was bright green. It studied the other finch and shook its feathers.

"Mr. Darby," Megan said, "the last few times we saw Charlie Red, he looked . . . different."

"Like a caricature of Charlie!" Richie injected. "Or like a mannequin—or one of those creepy wax mummies— made up to look like Charlie. And his hair was so red . . . it was like it was on fire!"

Mr. Darby grunted in a way that made Noah and the rest of the scouts nervous.

"What is it?" Noah asked.

"We're concerned that DeGraff . . ." His voice trailed off, as if he couldn't bear to say what came next. "We're afraid he has poisoned Charlie as well."

Ella sat up straight, and Richie's eyes grew almost as big as the lenses in his glasses.

Noah said, "We've talked about DeGraff changing animals—but never *people!*"

"Council has always feared the possibility."

"Will he go after others?" Noah asked.

Mr. Darby frowned. "One of our security guards is missing. Shortly after the incident with Charlie, he disappeared."

As the train steamed out of Arctic Town, Mr. Darby lifted the finches and gently tossed them out the window, where they flew off in opposite directions, marking the gray sky with spots of color. They rode past PizZOOria, the Forest of Flight, and several other exhibits.

A minute later, the engineer applied the brakes and the train shuddered on the tracks. Mr. Darby stepped out onto a wooden platform, saying, "Come! Come! Let's go!" and the scouts piled out and fell in line behind him.

Mr. Darby hurried the short distance to Giraffic Jam. His walk was slightly uneven, and at one point he stumbled and brushed against the leafless twigs of an overgrown bush.

"What the heck . . ." said Ella.

Noah glanced over and shrugged.

At Giraffic Jam, Mr. Darby pushed aside the "Closed for Construction!" sign and made his way into the building, bumping his head on the open door. Inside, he quickly climbed off the winding wooden deck and strode out across the exhibit, not bothering to greet the giraffes.

"Come!" he called out, but the scouts were already on his heels.

"Mr. Darby?" Noah said. "You . . . ummm . . . okay?"

"Yes, yes, fine!" His voice was now as rushed as the rest of him.

As they stepped up to a particular giraffe, he said, "Lofty, please!" The giraffe stared down at the old man and finished chewing on a wad of leaves. Then he lumbered over to a thin waterfall and stuck his head through it. A second later, the ground rumbled and a platform slowly began to rise from it, dirt raining off its edges. Lofty had thrown a lever.

"One of my preferred gateways," Mr. Darby explained. "I'm too old to be crawling through tunnels and riding waterslides."

Mr. Darby took the scouts down a quick flight of steps that led down into the hole the platform had revealed. Then he took them into a corridor with four branches: the Grottoes—gateways into the Secret Zoo. One branch had a velvet curtain, and a sign above it read "The Secret Giraffic Jam." The scouts followed Mr. Darby through the curtain and out onto a wooden deck in a sector of the Secret Zoo. A man with a mohawk and a leather jacket with velvet patches was standing nearby. A Descender, an older one than the scouts were used to dealing with.

"Mr. Darby," he said, "I have—"

The old man hushed him with a wave of his hand. Then he stumbled over to the deck railing and met a giraffe's gaze.

"Aerial—my jacket, please."

Aerial took a few steps and craned her long neck into a tree. Mr. Darby's velvet jacket was draped across a branch, and the giraffe worked her head under it. Then she swung down her neck, delivering it to Mr. Darby, who quickly pushed his arms through the sleeves after taking off his other jacket.

"Mr. Darby?" the Descender said.

The old man, his back to the Descender, held a single finger into the air. Then he leaned his hands onto the rail like someone catching his breath. Seconds passed.

Beneath her breath, Ella sang, "Awk-waarrd . . ."

Mr. Darby finally turned around to face the Descender. "Yes?" he said in his familiar, friendly tone, as if nothing unusual had just happened.

"Sir . . . I'm afraid we have a problem."

"And what is it?"

The Descender opened his mouth, and then closed it. His eyes shifted one way, and then another. "Perhaps you should come with me, sir."

CHAPTER 4

THE MESSAGE

The scouts and Mr. Darby followed the Descender out of the Secret Giraffic Jam and across Species Park and its wild assortment of animals: bears, koalas, orangutans. They turned onto the streets of the City of Species and hurried across its brightly colored sidewalks, stepping over streams and dodging the feathered rumps of peacocks. They cut through alleys, through the Library of the Secret Society, and through the wavering shadow beneath the Wotter Tower.

"Over there!" the Descender said, and Noah looked where he was pointing—the main entrance into the

Secret Creepy Critters. A large group of animals and people had gathered there.

Mr. Darby hollered, *"Move! Move!"* as he stepped through the crowd, bumping aside anything in his path. As he and the scouts made it to the front, Noah saw what everyone was interested in. Boots, a hat, two jackets, and a backpack lay on the ground. They belonged to Tameron, Sam, and Hannah—the Descenders trapped by DeGraff.

A young teenager hurried over. He had bright blue eyes and hair shaved so short that it looked like the stubble of a days-old beard. Another Descender. Mr. Darby reached down to the pile of things and lifted a boot. Purple leather. Hannah's.

"Derek . . ." Mr. Darby said to the young Descender. "These things . . . When did they get here?"

"Ten minutes ago. Fifteen, maybe."

"From the portal?"

Derek nodded. "It just opened and everything flew out."

"Did you see anyone?"

The young Descender shook his head.

"Any demands?" Mr. Darby asked. "Was there a letter?"

"No—no message."

Mr. Darby dropped the boot and picked up a tight-fitting knit hat with a short brim. Tameron's. "The clothing . . . it is the message."

"Huh?"

The old man set the hat back onto the pile. "DeGraff wants us to know that our friends no longer have their gear. Send the crowd away. Pull some Descenders from their posts and close off the city streets for a five-block radius."

"Yes, sir." Derek turned and began to wave away the crowd, which went compliantly.

Noah watched Mr. Darby put his foot on the canvas backpack to feel the hard, winding coils of Tameron's tail. Then the old man looked to the velvet curtains—their bright sheen, their vertical folds, their tassels.

He clenched his hands and took a step toward the curtain. "What do you want?" He spoke softly, more to himself than to the man hidden somewhere inside the sector. "Why have you come back?"

But Noah himself already knew the answer. DeGraff was here to conquer the Secret Zoo.

Mr. Darby abruptly turned and headed off, almost stepping on the tail of a wandering platypus. "Come!" he said to the scouts. "We must hurry—now more than ever!"

CHAPTER 5

THE ROOM OF REFLECTIONS

The scouts gazed up at the library, a twenty-story, octagonal building capped with a stained-glass dome. It had taken little more than ten minutes to get here from the Secret Creepy Critters, and on their way they'd been joined by Solana, a Descender and a good friend of Sam, Tameron, and Hannah—DeGraff's hostages. Some of the animals that the scouts knew also came along: Podgy, an emperor penguin capable of flying; P-Dog and his coterie of rambunctious prairie dogs; and Marlo, who'd taken his usual perch on Noah's shoulder.

Inside, tall trees and towering bookcases shared the

large, open space. Shelves were fastened to tree trunks, and rows of books were lined up along horizontal branches. Monkeys in vests climbed up and down, pulling books for patrons.

"This way," said Mr. Darby.

They hung a left and came to a glass elevator big enough to fit them all, Podgy beside Mr. Darby and the prairie dogs racing around everyone's feet. As they rose, Noah stared down at the passing balconies and at people lounging in pillowed chairs, sipping from steamy mugs, their attention buried in thick books. Dozens of monkeys were climbing around, plucking books from shelves like fruit from branches.

Within a minute, the marble walls of the library turned to glass, and Noah realized the elevator had ascended into the domed roof. As the world exploded with bright light, the scouts squinted out across the City of Species, and Noah saw the pillars of the Wotter Tower, the hard walls of Metr-APE-olis, and a narrow wing of the Secret Creepy Critters, which weaved through the other buildings like a wild branch of ivy.

The elevator doors parted and everyone exited onto a clear floor that made a room of the top of the dome. The walls were stained glass.

Noah looked down. The glass floor was so spotless that it felt like they were standing in the air.

"Okay . . ." Ella said, "now this is kind of freaky."

Richie said, "Are . . . are we confident this floor can support all of us at once?"

"Us and a lot more," Solana said.

In the middle of the room were more than a dozen men and women seated in glass chairs. They were members of the Secret Council—Noah could tell by their velvet coats. Off to one side was Evie, the leader of the Specters, six girls who could blend themselves into their surroundings by using chameleons and magic. She was sitting with one leg drawn up against her on a table made entirely of glass. Her long bangs were draped over the better part of her face, and she was twisting a drawstring on her hooded sweatshirt.

The chairs were all facing the same direction, away from the elevator. Mr. Darby quietly led the scouts to a place in front of the group, and then held his arms out, saying, "The Room of Reflections."

Noah wondered why it was called that, but didn't ask.

Mr. Darby swept an open palm toward Evie. "I've asked the leader of the Specters to also join us today. And Solana will be representing the Descenders."

Evie did nothing to acknowledge the scouts or Solana. She continued to sit on the table, twirling her drawstring around and around her finger.

"We only await the arrival of Zak."

"Zak?" Noah asked.

"A Teknikal. He should be here any—"

Ding!

The doors to a second glass elevator parted, and out wafted a cloud of smoke. A figure appeared—a young teenage boy waving an arm in front of his face. He stepped out of the elevator pulling a wobbly cart behind him. The cart had a metal plate with "Don't touch! Property of Teknikals!" engraved on it.

"Zak?" Mr. Darby said. "Is there a problem?"

The boy shook his head. As the smoke cleared, Zak came into full view. His blue overalls and white T-shirt, both streaked with oil and smeared with soot, sagged on his skinny frame. He had a crooked, unkempt Mohawk and round goggles with tinted lenses and a wide rubber strap. As he pulled his squeaky cart near the scouts, he tripped once on his own feet, then opened one of the cart doors and ducked his head inside.

"Where's all the smoke coming from?" Richie asked.

"Ohhh . . . that's nothing, bro," Zak answered as he nosily fumbled around for something, his voice echoing in the confined space of the cart. "Another project."

Mr. Darby raised an eyebrow over his sunglasses and said, "I hope that's not the project for the Conservation Committee" in a tone that was uncharacteristically stern.

Zak stayed silent in a way that communicated it was.

"I trust you'll have it working soon?"

Zak stayed silent again, this time to show he wasn't sure.

"Zak?"

"Have I ever let you down, Mr. D?"

Mr. Darby frowned and dropped his eyebrow behind his sunglasses.

After a few seconds, a squeal emitted from the cart and the smoke stopped at once. Zak's head emerged. He pulled off his dirty goggles, spat onto each lens, and wiped them on the cleanest spot on his T-shirt. Then he clapped his goggles back onto his face and grinned.

"Eww," Ella whispered into Megan's ear. "Please don't ever let him touch me."

Zak scratched a spot on his skinny rear end, then plunged his head back into the cabinet. With him out of sight, each of the scouts turned to Mr. Darby with worried looks.

"He's a bit unorthodox," Mr. Darby said apologetically, "but the Teknikals are very good at what they do, I assure you."

"What you call 'unorthodox,' I call 'smelly,'" Ella said. "And what is it that the Teknikals do, anyway?"

"This . . ." Zak said as he held out his arm. In his hand was a tiny video camera with a dozen lens tubes the size of quarter rolls looking off in different ways. Each lens

was as multicolored as the stained glass around them. Several small straps with steel buckles dangled below the camera.

Zak smiled, revealing a silver tooth.

Mr. Darby turned to the scouts and explained. "The Teknikals are exceptionally skilled in technology. And with the help of our magical scientists, they've developed ways to incorporate the Secret Zoo's magic into their contraptions. There's almost nothing the Teknikals can't create."

Richie said, "Way . . . way . . . *way* cool . . ."

Ella rolled her eyes. "Show Zak your nerd-gear, why don't you?" When Richie reached for his shirt pocket, Ella added, "I'm kidding, you freak."

"It's a camera," Mr. Darby said, referring to what Zak was holding. "The image it produces is like nothing you've seen."

"Wow!" Richie said. "Let me see!"

"Oh . . . you're going to see, bro," Zak said. "We're *all* about to see."

Ella leaned toward Megan and said, "What's up with the 'bro' thing? This guy related to everyone?"

Megan only shrugged, and from her seat on the table, Evie chuckled.

Noah glanced at Evie, Solana, and Zak. Three young teenagers from three different groups using magic to do extraordinary things. The Specters, the Descenders, the Teknikals. The Secret Zoo never stopped surprising.

Mr. Darby turned to the scouts. "Shortly after Sam and the others were captured, I received a message from DeGraff. The note said so very little that it seemed only to confirm DeGraff's whereabouts in the Secret Zoo. It was practically an invitation for the Secret Society to storm into the Creepy Critters sector. And why would DeGraff want that, if not to trick us?"

Noah thought about this. It made sense. How many times had DeGraff had the upper hand? Just days ago, he'd fooled the Secret Society into believing Charlie Red was him, luring the Crossers into the cellar beneath Clarksville Elementary, setting the trap to capture Sam, Hannah, and Tameron.

Mr. Darby continued, "Council immediately met to discuss a course of action. We wondered about secretly sending in an animal to survey the sector. It would have to be a Gifted, of course, so that it could understand its mission. And it would have to be small enough to stay hidden. After much deliberation, we decided on Marlo. We needed to see what he saw, and an ROR camera was our first thought."

"Huh?" Ella said, squinting.

"Sorry," Mr. Darby said. "ROR—*Room of Reflections*." He gestured around him again.

Zak lifted his arm with the camera in his open palm, and a tuft of armpit hair shot out from under the short sleeve of his shirt.

"This morning, we strapped it onto Marlo and sent him on his way. He soon returned—*safely*, thank heavens. None of us have seen the footage yet."

After a pause, Mr. Darby looked again to Zak. "Are we ready?"

Zak wiped a smudge off his reflective goggles with his T-shirt. "Just say the word and I'll press go."

Mr. Darby looked over at the crowd. "Does anyone have concerns before we begin?" When no one spoke up, he turned again to Zak, saying, "You may . . . *press go.*"

The few council members that were standing found their seats, and Solana and the scouts moved in behind them.

Zak crouched in front of the group and, with two loud clicks, fixed the camera onto a floor mount, the only item Noah could see in the room that wasn't made of glass. The lenses began to roll and shift, each independent of the others, like eyes of chameleons.

"Scouts," Mr. Darby said, "I almost forgot—try not to stare into the lenses."

The floor mount began to swivel left and right. A beam of light shot from a lens into the air, struck the stained glass above, and instead of passing through, bounced back in dozens of directions, reflecting color all around. Light streamed out from a second lens and hit a new spot along the ceiling in the same way. A third beam rose. Then a fourth, a fifth—more and more until all the lenses were casting light.

Noah looked down at himself. His body seemed a canvas for colors to collect upon. His clothes went from purple to green to blue. A blur of different hues moved across Podgy and the prairie dogs, who'd gathered to one side.

The camera began to spin on the floor mount. The bright beams began to spread and blend into one another.

Soft popping noises came from all around.

"Speakers," Zak explained. He pointed above his head. "Tiny things—they're mounted all around. The camera's equipped with several mics. Marlo . . . he picked up every sound when he was in there."

The noise of a steady wind began to fill the room, and something to the left of the scouts began to take shape—leafy limbs and brown bark. To the scouts' right, more trees appeared. What remained of the glass ceiling became a canopy of leaves outlined in patches of blue sky. A sophisticated, virtual world was closing in around them in perfect 3-D. In the glass floor, tree branches appeared above a distant city street, and animals seemed to stroll past—lions, bears, and ostriches. A group of giraffes were reaching their long necks to snack on leaves.

The virtual world dipped and turned. Marlo swerved through a batch of koalas nestled in the tree limbs, and then barely missed crashing into a sloth, which dangled upside down, its curved claws wrapped around a branch.

"I'm going to puke!" Richie said.

"Then point your mouth away from me!" Ella answered.

As the virtual world tilted, Noah reached out to brace himself before remembering he wasn't actually moving. City places came into view: the Secret Metr-APE-olis, Platypus Playground, and a giant fountain with beady streams of water standing hundreds of feet high. The kingfisher swerved to avoid a balcony, and then flew down a narrow alley, birds scattering. He streamed through a cloud of hummingbirds, then through a cloud of mist. As he soared past the glass walls of Butterfly Nets, one side of the Room of Reflections seemed to crowd with butterflies, and Noah almost believed he could reach out and touch their papery wings.

Ella half shouted over the sound of the wind, "Beats IMAX, huh?" and Noah turned to see she was holding on to the chair in front of her.

"Don't barf, don't barf, don't barf," Richie softly chanted.

The Secret Creepy Critters came into view. The center of the building, the Creepy Core, rose as high as ten stories before ending at a concrete dome. Dozens of wings reached out in all directions, snaking between trees and other structures like the tentacles of a stone octopus. Dead ivy covered the walls and the grass around the sector had wilted and turned black.

"See the ground?" Mr. Darby asked. Noah turned to the voice and found Mr. Darby and the rest of the Secret Council seeming to fly through the treetops. "The Shadowist has caused that. His existence is like a disease."

Marlo swooped down toward the entrance, where two Descenders that Noah didn't recognize stood guard. An instant later, the kingfisher plunged between two velvet curtains, gated into the sector, and cast the entire Room of Reflections into absolute darkness.

Richie shrieked.

Mr. Darby's voice rose in the dark: "Richie? I trust all is well, yes?"

"And I'm trusting no one got barfed on," Ella cut in.

"I'm okay," Richie answered. "My bad—sorry."

"Can anyone see anything?" a woman from the Secret Council asked.

A chorus of no's came.

"Shh!" someone said—Noah thought it had been Solana. "You guys hear that?"

Everyone became deathly quiet. In the recorded world, a low, rumbling growl sounded—the unmistakable noise of a sasquatch. A second growl came. Then a third, a fourth.

Noah peered into the blackness all around him and couldn't see a thing—not the faintest suggestion of light. "Did we lose video?"

"Negative," Zak answered. "System's still live, bro. We're seeing exactly what Marlo saw."

As the growls faded, it was obvious that Marlo was flying down the corridor, away from the velvet curtains. A dimly lit passage appeared as Marlo turned in the virtual world, and above an open doorway, a sign read, "Bugs-A-Bunch." The Creepy Critters exhibit in the Clarksville Zoo had a corridor with the same name—the one Marlo was now entering was its magical counterpart.

Walls of broken aquariums were covered in a writhing mass of spiders, millipedes, and cockroaches. Some were fighting; others were chomping on fallen prey. Cobwebs and cocoons dangled from the ceiling.

A sasquatch sat against one wall. Hunched over its knees, it seemed to be waiting. Countless insects had their long legs and segmented bodies tangled in its mangy fur.

"Okay . . ." Ella said, her voice quivering a bit, "this movie we're watching? Yeah, it just went to PG-13 *really* fast."

Marlo flew past the sasquatch undetected, came to a three-way intersection, and turned down a new corridor. At another intersection, Marlo turned at an open door with a sign reading, "Fish Foyer." Most of the aquariums were still intact and filled with fish, but a few were broken, their dark holes surrounded by pointed pieces of glass, looking like the gaping mouths of monsters.

A sasquatch sat on the floor, its back against the wall. It seemed to be waiting, just like the other.

"How come that thing doesn't see Marlo?" someone from the Secret Council asked.

Mr. Darby answered, "Marlo's blending in with the flying insects."

This made sense to Noah. At least half of the insects were as big or bigger than the tiny kingfisher, even with the camera on his back.

As Marlo made a turn into a new corridor, a cockroach flew straight toward a camera lens, and in the Room of Reflections, it grew and grew until its stringy antennae became the size of tree trunks. It banged off the lens and everyone shrieked, including the Secret Council, who also ducked down in their chairs, arms raised around their heads. Once it was obvious what had happened, sighs of relief sounded and people eased back up in their seats.

In a squeaky voice, Richie said, "New underpants, please."

A sign read, "Legless Lane" as Marlo made a turn. Swells of snakes slithered across the floor and one another. To Noah, they looked like a spill of giant spaghetti noodles.

"Oh . . . Emm . . . Gee," Ella said. Dozens of cobras had

reared up into the air, their hooded necks spread out.

When Legless Lane came to an end, Marlo quickly found a perch in an area that looked like a massive cavity within a mountain. A few thin waterfalls trickled down from the heights, splashing into murky streams. Occasional aquariums were set in the rocky walls. Much larger than the ones in the corridors, these might have once contained alligators, crocodiles, and komodo dragons. But now their glass walls were broken.

"The Creepy Core," Mr. Darby said.

Spiders and millipedes and other unnameable bugs were crawling around on the mostly open floor.

Marlo suddenly fluttered a few feet over to a new perch. Beside him was a tarantula—or what had once been a tarantula, anyway. Now it was twice its normal size: its legs as large as a small king crab's; its body as plump as a peach; its oversized eyes like a cluster of black marbles.

"Is that a spider?" Ella asked. "If you haven't noticed, it's the size of a poodle."

The tarantula lunged at Marlo, who flew safely into the air. As the spider came down, it struggled to cling to the rocky wall and then tumbled over a ledge.

Members of the Secret Council turned to one another, nervous conversations breaking out.

"What?" Noah asked. "What is it? What's wrong?"

It was Mr. Darby who answered. "That tarantula . . . it

was poisoned by DeGraff. It was turned into . . . something . . . by his dark magic, like the sasquatches."

"And how many others have been?" a woman from the Secret Council asked.

Mr. Darby stayed silent, as if afraid to guess.

Noah looked down at the animals on the floor and felt goose bumps rise along his arms. The body of a particular snake went on and on. Noah counted ten feet, twenty feet, thirty feet, more. Was it a python? Or was it a smaller snake made monstrous by the Shadowist?

Marlo darted over to a large pit surrounded by glass walls and capped by a glass ceiling. The space in the ground contained a few small trees, a trickling waterfall, a shallow pool, and a dirt floor with patches of long, sickly grass.

"The Croc Crater," Megan said, and Noah realized they were looking at the magical counterpart to the crocodile exhibit in the Clarksville Zoo.

Marlo landed on top of the glass roof beside an air vent. Deep in the pit were Tank and the three Descenders. The Secret Council gasped and sat up in their seats.

"There!" Mr. Darby called out in case anyone hadn't noticed. "You see!"

Marlo was frightened into the air by a sudden swarm of monstrous hornets, and he flew to a nearby spot on a freestanding rock covered with cave crickets. Here he had another view into the pit. He chirped once, twice, trying in vain to get the attention of his friends.

Tank slumped against one wall, his bald head spotted with grime. Hannah sat with her knees pulled up to her chest, her legs wrapped in her arms. Sam and Tameron seemed to be asleep on the dirt floor. Their faces were gaunt.

In the Room of Reflections, Solana stepped toward the image of her friends. "Why don't they break out?" she asked. "Why don't they climb a tree and smash the glass or something?"

"They can't," Mr. Darby said. "Not without their Descender gear—you know that. The glass is too strong." He moved to a spot near Solana and pointed down into the pit, where one wall wasn't visible from Marlo's position. "The only way in or out is through a locked door on this side, the side we can't see."

"Are you sure?" Solana asked.

Mr. Darby nodded. "I'm almost certain. In the Clarksville Zoo, the Croc Crater has a similar door. When I first designed it—"

Mr. Darby stopped abruptly. Noah rewound the old man's words in his head and let them play a second time. Had Mr. Darby designed the zoo?

Evie and the other Secret Cityzens were staring curiously at Mr. Darby.

Mr. Darby said, "I . . ." His voice trailed off. Then he suddenly diverted his attention to the virtual world, where Marlo had flown back to the ceiling of the glass enclosure. He pointed a shaky finger into the pit and said, "There! You see the door!"

Everyone turned their attention back to the video.

Megan said, "How do we—"

The virtual world began to whirl. Forgetting it wasn't real, Noah reached out and braced himself on a chair. Marlo, who had been tumbling through the air, flew straight again, stabilizing the camera.

"Behind us!" someone from the Secret Council called out.

Everyone turned around to see the image of a sasquatch, its wicked stare locked on them. In the virtual world, the beast seemed four times its already enormous size. Apparently it had just taken a swing at Marlo, knocking him off his perch.

Marlo turned back the way he had come. The sasquatch swiped at him a second time and missed, flying insects becoming entangled in the fur of his arm. As Marlo flew off, the sasquatch chased after him, crunching across bugs. A snake bit into its heel and was dragged along, its body whipping left and right.

Noah glanced to one side and saw a large window looking into a room. A man was standing inside, staring out at the commotion while holding a key chain attached to a string. Red hair, big freckles, lanky limbs—Charlie Red. As Marlo flew off, Noah noticed two doors on either side of the window; the left one went into Charlie's room, and the right was marked "Lower Level."

Marlo flew down Legless Lane and veered into a new corridor. Back in Fish Foyer, the sasquatch on guard lunged for him and barely missed. Noah glanced back to see the beast slam into the opposite wall, breaking glass. Water burst into the air. Seconds later, the beast pulled itself from the cavity it had made, fish flopping at its feet. It spotted Marlo, then joined the other sasquatch in the chase.

"Two sasquatches now!" someone from the council announced.

"Yes," Mr. Darby answered in a flat tone. "There will be others."

Marlo turned down a bug-filled corridor, and a third sasquatch dropped from an opening in the ceiling to join the pursuit.

"I can't take this!" Richie declared.

Noah turned to see that his friend had pulled down the ribbed cuff of his cap, blinding himself and reminding Noah of how a frightened turtle ducks its head into its shell.

Marlo flew down a new corridor, then another. He

veered through openings in the green, ropey vines that dangled from the ceiling, mosquitoes and flies showering across his body. As he headed down a particularly dark hall, the point of light at the end of it seemed to be narrowing.

Noah squinted into Marlo's world. "What's happening?"

Marlo picked up speed. As the walls whizzed by, Noah realized the passage at the end of the hall was closing.

"A trap," Mr. Darby said.

Marlo neared the end of the corridor, and the watchers saw how a steel wall was being lowered from the ceiling. The opening was reduced to four feet, three feet, two feet. Marlo dipped down and flew near the floor, his wings brushing the backs of the insects there. Seconds before the gap closed, he plunged through, and steel clattered and clanked as at least one sasquatch crashed into the wall.

Within seconds, a new sasquatch pounced at Marlo, trying to stamp on him. As the kingfisher flew back into the heights, the sasquatch chased after him on all fours. Something fell from the ceiling—a net. Marlo tucked in his wings and squirted through an opening in the cords, and the net closed around the sasquatch, knocking it to its knees.

Noah glanced around. Megan was clutching her chest; Ella had her hands pressed to her mouth; Richie had come out from under his cap and was gazing out with wide eyes. Prairie dogs were huddled behind Podgy. The Secret Council was frowning and shaking their heads.

In a new corridor, a series of trap doors swung open, hordes of insects spilling like water into their dark depths. Marlo passed easily above the danger and turned down a new corridor.

The Room of Reflections again fell into darkness, and from somewhere ahead came the low growl of several sasquatches. Noah realized Marlo was in the corridor leading back to the City of Species. The portal came into view, a sliver of light. Seconds passed. The growls shifted from the front of the room to the back as Marlo flew past his adversaries. A few seconds later, the kingfisher shot through the crevice between the two curtains.

The virtual world exploded with light. Trees and buildings blurred past, and the room filled with the sounds of the city. As a building that Noah had never seen came into view, the kingfisher veered toward it, then down to the ground, where Zak and Mr. Darby appeared. Zak walked over to him and reached out his arm. There was a loud *click!*—the power button being pushed—and then both sound and sight in the three-dimensional world exploded with static—a noisy storm of black and white dots. As the scouts poked their fingers into their ears, Zak jumped up to the camera and hit a switch, instantly returning the glass walls in the Room of Reflections to normal.

All eyes turned to Mr. Darby. The old man took a deep breath, pulled back his shoulders, and adjusted his jacket. Then he stared out at the group through his dark sunglasses and said, "It seems our nemesis has been back for a long time."

✿ CHAPTER 6 ✿

THE SCOUTS STEP UP

Though Noah couldn't hear what Mr. Darby was saying to Evie, it was obvious that they were disagreeing. On the other side of the Room of Reflections, the old man was leaning toward her, his long beard dancing in the open space between them as he talked. Evie stood with her arms crossed, a bend in one knee, her hip cocked out to the side.

After seeing Marlo's video, the Secret Council had collectively agreed it would be foolish to charge into the Secret Creepy Critters. Every corridor was a bottleneck—too narrow for an effective assault. Too many traps had been set, and too many sasquatches were standing guard. And of the millions of insects, how many might attack, if their allegiance was now to DeGraff? When there was mention of a covert action to rescue the four captives, everyone fell silent. Then Mr. Darby had asked for a private moment with Evie.

The Secret Cityzens broke up into small groups to talk among themselves. Solana and Zak were hunched over the Teknikal's cart, studying the camera that had recorded Marlo's dangerous travels. The scouts were gathered around their animal friends. The prairie dogs were running around in circles, energized, it seemed, by the incredible view through the glass floor.

Megan gave a subtle, sideways nod toward Evie and Mr. Darby. "What's that all about?"

"What do you *think* it's about?" Ella said as she batted her ponytail off her shoulder with a flick of her wrist. "A second after a secret mission gets mentioned, Mr. Darby walks off with Invisigirl."

Noah turned his attention back to Solana and happened to see Zak reach one of his puny arms around his backside and pull the seat of his overalls out from the crack of his rear end.

"So . . . *ewww*," Ella said, and Noah realized she'd seen, too. She scrunched up her face and added, "That dude is too weird."

A few minutes later, Evie and Mr. Darby walked back over to the rest of the group. Everyone waited to hear what the Secret Society leader had to say.

Mr. Darby cleared his throat and announced, "Evie has agreed to attempt to rescue our friends."

"By herself?" one of the council members asked.

"She'll take another Specter to help her carry the Descenders' gear." Mr. Darby had already shared the story of discovering the Descenders' items outside of the Secret Creepy Critters.

"When?"

"Saturday night."

An older man with a bushy handlebar mustache said, "Pardon me, Mr. Darby, but isn't that the same date planned for the rescue of Blizzard and Little Bighorn? Won't Evie be needed there?"

"Evie's agreed to split up her team. One Specter will go with her, the other four will go with Solana and"—he looked over to the scouts—"our friends from the Outside, I am hoping."

Ella took a step back, and Richie grabbed for his heart.

"Us!" Richie said. "*Us?* When did—"

"My apologies, Richie," Mr. Darby said. "I hadn't meant for the topic to arise this way."

The man with the big mustache said, "They don't know?"

"I'm afraid not."

"Know *what*?" Richie asked.

Mr. Darby turned his entire body toward the scouts. "My primary reason for inviting you here today is ask you a question." He paused and rubbed his chin. "Would you be willing to join us in the attempt to rescue Blizzard and Little Bighorn?"

Richie gasped, but the other scouts hardly flinched.

"Council has already spoken on the matter," Mr. Darby went on, "and we feel the four of you are needed. Our two Gifteds have been shot, tranquilized, and imprisoned. There's no telling what emotional state they'll be in.

"Despite their intelligence, Blizzard and Little Bighorn are still animals. The four of you can help calm them. They know you, they trust you. When I watch you with them, I see something beyond friendship—I see something close to family. They'll feel your love, and it'll keep them peaceful."

Mr. Darby was right. Noah thought of all the adventures he'd spent with Blizzard—the times they'd spent crosstraining, and even sleeping side-by-side in Arctic Town and the Forest of Flight. They'd risked their own lives to protect each other, Blizzard in the Dark Lands, Noah in his school gymnasium just days ago.

Mr. Darby said, "They're your special friends. Ours, too. Help us to help them."

Noah looked over at the other scouts. If they were caught breaking into the Waterford Zoo, their lives would never be the same. Megan met Noah's eyes, and she nodded, her pigtails swinging on the sides of her head.

"Excellent," Mr. Darby said. "There is, of course, the matter of your parents."

"Sleepovers," Megan said at once. "On Saturday. I'll go to Ella's, and Noah can stay at Richie's. We'll sneak out once our parents go to sleep."

"You'll need to go in as ghosts," Mr. Darby said. "Specters."

"But . . . how?" Noah said.

"There are twelve pairs of portal pants in existence—two pairs for each Specter. Four will go on loan to you. Evie—how long will it take you to train the scouts to use your gear?"

Evie looked out from beneath her bangs with one eye. "We can do the basics in two sessions. Three, tops. I can get them to ghost, but that's about it."

"Of course," Mr. Darby said. "I don't expect them to mirage."

Megan looked over to Noah and mouthed, *Mirage?* Noah just shrugged.

Mr. Darby's smile broadened. "Excellent! Plan to meet Evie and her companions tomorrow in Butterfly Nets. In the meantime, Council will review the layout of the

Waterford Zoo, and study Marlo's video to come up with a safe passage into the Creepy Core. As for right now, I'm afraid the four of you need to get home. You've already been here—"

"Wait!" Noah said. "I noticed something in the video that might be important. You guys saw Charlie Red, right?"

Almost everyone nodded, frowning.

"Did you see the doors—the ones next to the room he was in?" When no one responded, Noah added, "One of them was marked 'Lower Level.' It must be a staircase, and I bet it goes to the Croc Crater door, the one that's kept locked."

"Hmmm . . ." Mr. Darby said. "I wonder if our old friend Charlie has the key."

Noah nodded. "He was swinging his key chain . . . in the video."

"Hold on," Megan said. "We already have a key—the magic one! The one we use for the Clarksville Zoo!"

Mr. Darby shook his head. "That key was designed to only work in the Outside. A safety mechanism imposed by Council." To Noah, he said, "Thank you. We'll review the video again for more clues."

Noah nodded once more, and the scouts and their animal companions were led across the Room of Reflections. Evie, Solana, and the Secret Council watched them go.

After stepping onto the elevator, they swung around to face Mr. Darby.

"You should know something," Mr. Darby said. "Wearing the Specters' gear isn't like wearing anything in the world—yours or mine."

"How?" Richie asked, a hint of worry in his tone.

Instead of answering Richie's question, Mr. Darby said, "Thank you, all—thank you for your commitment to us, and to the animals you love."

Before Noah could respond, the glass doors of the elevator sealed shut and the scouts plummeted into the depths of the majestic library in the ever-changing world of the Secret Zoo.

CHAPTER 7

NOAH'S NOISY CLOSET

Noah sat at his bedroom window, looking out at the night. Silhouettes of houses and treetops rose against a star-spotted sky. He couldn't stop thinking about the video from Zak's camera: the sasquatches, the throngs of insects, the dark corridors of the Secret Creepy Critters. He worried about Tank and the other Descenders in that wretched pit in the Creepy Core. He wondered about training with the Specters tomorrow—what it would be like to walk around as one of them, a ghost.

Around midnight, he left the window and climbed into bed. He tossed and turned, and eventually began to settle. Just as he drifted toward sleep, a sudden noise jarred him awake—a heavy groan.

He lifted his head and checked his bedroom door. It was still closed tight. In the moonlight, he could see the poster on the back of it. Indiana Jones seemed to look out at him, a coiled whip at his side and a wry grin on his face.

Noah squinted at the line of light along the bottom of his door, expecting to see the silhouette of a foot. Was his mother awake? His father? Was Megan also having troubles sleeping? When nothing appeared, he laid his head back down and forced his eyes closed. The old frame of the house settled and shifted at night—it had for years—and this was surely what Noah had heard.

A minute passed, and then Noah heard the groan again, louder this time. But his door was still closed and nothing showed in the light beneath it. Indy's grin now seemed scornful, as if the adventurer couldn't believe what a wimp Noah was being.

As soon as Noah's head returned to the pillow, the sound came again. This time he sat up, his senses at full attention. Nothing at the door; nothing at the window. He was alone.

He waited, his fingers curled around the edge of the mattress. His eyes shifted to random points in his room: the desk, the bookshelf, the dresser, the closet.

The closet.

Could the noise be coming from there?

Go to it, Noah heard the braver part of himself say in his head. *Just look inside—there's nothing there.*

He started to rise from the bed and fear stopped him short. What if someone *was* in his closet?

Noah recalled the portal beneath Clarksville Elementary. If DeGraff could build a portal to the old cellar in Noah's school, what was preventing him from building one to somewhere else—this room, even?

His heart was no longer tapping against his chest—it was thumping. His palms, suddenly clammy, stuck to his bedsheets.

The sound again, louder than ever. There was no doubt: the noise was coming from the closet.

Noah stood, his knees popping. He took one step, then another. When he reached the doorway, he peered inside. There was nothing but the usual: clothes dangling from hangers, sweaters half folded on shelves, a jumble of shoes. As he stepped inside, a wave of cold air rolled over him. He shivered, then reached up and tugged the chain for the light.

He listened for the sound. The night seemed quieter than ever. He began to hear the silence—a muffled drone in his ears.

He squatted beside the heat vent and held his palm an

inch away from it. Was the cold air coming from here? Noah wasn't sure, but it seemed to be. Maybe the sounds had come from here, too. Maybe the furnace was having problems.

Noah stood and abruptly walked out of the closet, angry at himself for allowing his imagination to run away. As if he didn't have enough real problems to deal with. . . . He crawled back into bed and rolled onto his side.

He lay there for the next half hour, his eyes shut and all his attention in his ears. The groan didn't come again. It was as if whatever had made the sound knew Noah was listening for it and had decided to stay quiet.

Something suddenly came to Noah's mind, and he lay there trying to forget it. But the thought kept coming back . . . and back . . . and back.

A groan sounded a little like a growl.

CHAPTER 8

GOING GHOST

"Check these out," Evie said. "They're for the mission."

She reached into one of her nonmagical pockets, pulled out a small handful of tiny electrical pieces, and held them out for everyone to see. The scouts and all six of the Specters were standing in the Clarksville Zoo in Butterfly Nets, which was marked outside as "Closed for Construction!"

Noah dipped his head and gazed into her hand. "They . . . they look like bugs, but I can hardly see them."

"That's the idea."

The Specter threw the pieces into the air, and as they

hit the ground, they bounced a few times and then started to crawl, emitting a soft, steady light.

"Gift from Zak," she said. "Flashmites. To lead us through the dark passages."

"Awesome!" Richie said.

"Their power dies within a few minutes. And you don't have to worry about picking them up because they'll look like dead bugs."

Richie chased after one of the flashmites, its wide spray of light making the decals in his running shoes sparkle. He bent over, pinched the electronic bug between his fingers, and stood straight to study it. "Did Zak make it?"

"He makes everything," Evie answered.

"Except his way to the shower," Ella said, and she pinched her nose. When Richie shot her a scornful look, she added, "Sorry—didn't mean to make fun of your bro, bro."

The Crossers watched the flashmites crawl around until their power drained away, then Evie swept them up and stuffed them into her pocket.

"Okay," Evie said, "let's get started." She looked at the other Specters. "Girls, we ready?"

Noah glanced at the other Specters and saw them nod. Sara had a wild, punkish look with blond hair in a slender Mohawk that came to a four-inch point. Dark makeup circled her eyes and streaked toward her temples. Lee-Lee had big eyes with long, curved lashes and collar-length hair which curved to a point just below her chin. Kaleena had deep brown skin and long, braided hair. Jordynn had a bushy Afro that tapered near her neck. Elakshi had perfect olive skin and dark eyes.

Evie reached into a backpack and took out a wad of clothes. Pants. She threw a pair to each of the scouts. Richie's struck his face and then dangled around his neck like a scarf.

"String waists," Evie pointed out. "They should fit fine."

Noah held his by the waist and then whipped the legs forward like a wrinkled bedsheet. The camouflage pants had a bunch of pockets, including two large ones that zipped shut. Velvet patches were stitched to different places.

"I've always considered velvet and camouflage to be perfect complements," Ella said as she stared down at what she'd been given. "It's what all the girls are wearing this year."

"Should we put them on?" Richie asked.

Evie said, "Unless you want to walk around all day with chameleons stuffed in your underwear."

Noah and Richie found a private spot to change and rejoined the group.

Ella spun in a circle and asked the boys, "You like?" Her camouflage pants were pink, her favorite color.

"How did you manage that?" Richie asked.

Ella shrugged. "Jealous? Maybe you want to switch?"

"We've always had a pink pair," Evie said. "Call it lucky."

Ella turned a second time and stared down on the backs of her legs. "I call it fate."

"Okay, this is how they work," Evie said, and she opened her left zipper. A line of chameleons crawled out and spread across her body. Parts of Evie began to blend into her surroundings, and after a few seconds, she completely vanished. "Takes about twenty chameleons to camo up," she added, and when Noah heard the rip of a zipper, he realized she'd closed her pocket. "To send the chameleons back, open your right pocket." A zipper sounded again, and then Evie began to appear like a figure rising out of the fog. By the time she was fully visible, all her chameleons were gone.

"That's it?" Richie said.

Evie nodded and shrugged one shoulder.

"Seriously? That's the extent of your instruction?"

"Look, kid, we got four Crossers down, and two Gifteds locked up in what basically amounts to a prison. Our operations go live in two days. You think we got time to read a few books about this?"

Richie opened his mouth to say something and then closed it.

"Good," Evie said. "Now, who wants to go first?"

The scouts looked at one another, silent.

"No one?" Evie said. "Okay, then how about you all go at the same time?" She jingled the flat metal slider on the zipper of her left pocket. "Pinch and pull. The chameleons will do the rest. Again—they're trained for this. You're mostly along for the ride."

The scouts traded uneasy glances, then Noah asked his friends, "On three?"

Ella and Megan nodded. Richie did, too, at least a little.

Noah grabbed the slider and counted, "One . . . two . . . THREE!"

As Noah's zipper opened, he felt the patter of little feet up his leg and he looked down to see a line of chameleons streaming out from the velvet confines of his pocket. The chameleons' colors began to swirl and blur and change, and Noah began to disappear—parts of his arms, his legs, his torso. He was being blended into the world around him.

Richie whimpered, and Noah turned to see parts of his friends disappearing: Ella's legs, Megan's arms, Richie's running shoes. They looked like colorful drawings being erased from a page.

Noah watched the last of himself disappear as two chameleons circled his ankles. He felt perfectly fine—and perfectly invisible.

"I can't see my hands!" Richie squealed. "Or my arms . . . or my anything!"

"Too wicked!" Ella said.

Noah turned again to his friends and saw only trees and paths and butterflies.

"Ow!" Richie said. Noah looked toward the sound of his voice and saw a shimmer of movement as Richie's chameleons adjusted to new spots. "Who just punched me?"

Ella's sinister laugh served as an answer.

"Seriously—what's wrong with you?"

Ella laughed again. "I could really get used to this."

"Can you feel the chameleons?" Evie asked.

Noah realized he could. On his shoulders, his back, his legs, he felt the prick and push of little feet.

"There's one on my butt!" Richie squealed. When his friends started to laugh, he added, "I'm serious!"

"I don't . . . I don't understand this," Megan said. "The chameleons—how are they doing this?"

Evie said, "Chameleons have special cells with pigment that allows them to create color. Our magic modifies this pigment to create colors and tones in a big-time way. Then, as the chameleons blend into their surroundings, so do the things beneath them—at least if the chameleons want them to, because they control everything with their thoughts."

This idea, to Noah, seemed perfectly normal and totally

absurd, just like everything about the Secret Zoo.

"Okay," Evie said. "Left pocket calls the chameleons; right pocket sends them back. If you want a bunch of chameleons, just keep your left pocket open—they'll come and come, more than you can imagine." Evie tucked her bangs behind her ear and said, "Try moving around. Get the feel for it."

Noah took a few steps, looked around, and nearly lost his balance. Without sight of his body—his arms, his shoulders, the bridge of his nose—he felt a bit uncoordinated. And he felt a bit . . . unreal. It was as if he were drifting through space like a ghost—like a specter.

"Wave your arms," Evie said, and even demonstrated, her arms turning slow circles in front of her.

"They feel funny," Megan said.

"That's because you can't see them and your brain's freaking out. It's sending signals to every part of your body trying to figure out what's going on."

Evie had them walk forward, backward, sideways. She had them shuffle and jump and crouch. She made them kick their legs and punch the air. The scouts kept discussing how weird it was not to see parts of themselves. Noah wondered if being a Specter had less to do with the way you looked and more to do with the way you felt.

Evie said, "When a zipper's open, anything can portal through the pocket—sounds, smells."

"Hear that Richie?" Ella said. "No farts."

All the Specters smiled. Sara even laughed a bit.

After about fifteen minutes, Evie had them remove their camouflage. For this, the scouts simply unzipped their right pockets and allowed the chameleons to retreat. The four friends slowly appeared.

"Too wild," Richie said as he patted his pockets to ensure the chameleons weren't in them. Noah saw his friend for the first time in a while: his hat pulled down low on his forehead, his pants pulled up over his narrow waist and knobby ankles.

"Okay," Evie said, "camouflage yourselves again and come with me."

"Where are we going?" Noah asked.

She pointed to an outside wall of Butterfly Nets. "That way."

"We just came in from *that way*," Ella remarked.

"You're going out into the Clarksville Zoo, fully ghosted."

"*Whoa!*" Richie said. "Don't you think we need more time to—"

"Kid—there is no time. We only got a couple days to get this right."

The scouts traded glances. Evie was right. If they were going to rescue Tank and the other Descenders, they had to act fast and be bold.

CHAPTER 9

PERIL AT PENGUIN PALACE

"We're headed to Penguin Palace," Evie told the scouts as she ghosted herself. "I want to see if you guys can make it all the way around the exhibit without getting spotted."

Penguin Palace was home to a huge four-sided aquarium, glass walls reaching from the floor to the ceiling. In the aquarium was a mass of land topped with ice. A narrow channel of water surrounded the island, providing a place for penguins to swim.

"Shouldn't be too tough," Megan said. "Not if we stay to the back of the building."

Evie said, "The only ones at the back are going to be us—the Specters. The four of you are going to get as close as you can to the visitors. I'm talking inches. It'll be a great test to see how well you can stay ghosted."

"But—"

"No buts, kid," Evie said. "Now . . . ghost up and follow me."

"How?" Megan asked. "We can't even see you!"

"Follow my voice. If I'm not able to talk, I'll mark myself from time to time."

"Huh?" Richie said. "What do you mean, 'mark yourself'?"

"That's how we show our positions. We use our surroundings, mostly. Like this." A bright blue butterfly came away from a nearby bush with its wings open. It rose several feet and stayed there, unmoving. Then it flew off, a fluttery streak of color across a green backdrop. It had been perched on Evie's hand.

"Sometimes we'll force a chameleon to move over a few inches." Evie demonstrated, and Noah saw a ghostly swirl of movement somewhere along the place he guessed her shoulder to be. "Pay attention . . . you'll see me."

Noah nodded and then realized no one could see the gesture.

"Let's go," Evie said.

When she fell silent, Noah glanced around to figure out which direction she'd gone.

"Over here," said Evie. About ten feet to Noah's left, a leaf broke away from a branch, twirled in the air, then coasted to the ground. "Eyes and ears—totally alert at all times. A Specter is always focused."

As Noah headed up the path, he sensed the group around him: small swirls of air, body heat, and near-soundless scratches against the concrete. And he could make out their aromas: soaps, deodorants, skin.

"I smell armpit," Ella said. "'Fess up—who stinks?"

A few of the Specters chuckled.

"Richie?" Ella asked.

Richie said, "You know . . . it's nice not to look at her, but can't we do something about her voice?"

As they reached the end of the path, the exit door opened a crack and Noah guessed that Evie was peering out to ensure the coast was clear. Seconds later, it swung outward a few feet and stayed open as the line of Specters made their way through. Then Noah and the scouts followed. The air was cold, and a flurry of snowflakes dotted the cloudy sky. Noah reached up and pulled down the earflaps on his cap, causing a chameleon to move to a new place.

"Stay behind me," Evie said, and Noah saw the small puff of her breath a few feet away. "When we get close to someone, keep quiet and try not to breathe. Ready?"

"Hold up," Richie said. "What if . . . what if I got to pee?"

After a few seconds, Evie's voice rose into the silence: "Are you serious?"

"I'm just saying—I spent some time at the drinking fountain today."

"Stay out of the bathroom—too risky. Find a bush."

"I'm not worried about *that*."

"Then what's the problem?"

"Well . . . the chameleons . . . they crawl around, you know . . . and if I have to pull down my pants—" A smack sounded, and Richie finished his sentence with *"Oww!"*

"Seriously?!" Ella said. "With all that's at stake, you're worried about *that*?"

"I'm not *worried*!" Richie shot back. "I'm just . . . concerned! They have claws, you know. The last thing I need is—"

"Follow me and stay close," Evie interrupted. "With this snow, it'll be easy to mark me."

Noah quickly found out what she was referring to. Falling snowflakes traced the invisible curves of her body. Same with the other Specters and scouts. The effect in the snowfall was so subtle that Noah wouldn't have noticed had he not been looking for it. Evie turned down a path, avoided the snowy parts on a lawn, and pushed through the doors of Penguin Palace to step onto a wide mat in a narrow hallway.

"Wipe your feet," Evie whispered in the lowest voice imaginable. *"Quietly."*

As Noah softly dried the soles of his shoes, Evie continued, "Penguin Palace is a popular place—there's going to be visitors on every side. Get as close as you can to them and try to hold your position for a full minute. Then move on to the next room. You'll have to sense where you stand in relation to one another. Reach out with your fingers if you need to. Don't talk—unless you're in a corner away from people."

When Noah sensed that everyone was on the move, he walked out into a long room along the first side of the aquarium. A family of five stood against the glass wall, their gazes fixed on penguins swimming through the channel of water.

Someone brushed against his shoulder and he realized the Specters were moving to the back of the exhibit. He inched forward, feeling around him to ensure the other scouts were doing the same. As he stopped directly behind the family, someone gently bumped each of his sides and he realized his friends were near.

In front of him, a young boy with big dimples reached up and clapped his palm against the glass as a penguin swam by. Noah waited and counted the seconds. He realized he was holding his breath. He was so perfectly still that he became conscious of his own body—the weight of his head, the pull of his arms, the dangle of his fingers. As he silently counted "thirty-two," a noise came from the back of the room.

Clink!

It had been one of the Specters, no doubt—and no doubt making the noise on purpose.

The mother looked around. Her gaze landed right on Noah, who felt his muscles tense. He didn't move. Or breathe. Could the woman see him? Could she somehow make out his ghostly shape?

Worry erupted in Noah as he felt a chameleon move to a new spot on his shoulder. Had it marked him? The mother's eyes seemed to burrow into him. Pressure built in Noah's chest, and his heart began to tap against his sternum like something wanting out.

The woman frowned, puzzled, and then turned to watch her son smile at the sight of a new penguin. One of the scouts tugged Noah's sleeve and pulled him away from the aquarium and toward the end of the room.

In a corner, Richie whispered, "I practically pooped in there."

"That?" Evie whispered. "That was nothing."

"It sure felt like something to me," Ella said.

Evie dropped the topic by saying, "Everyone here?"

Each of the scouts whispered yes.

"Good," Evie said. "Let's go again."

Noah felt Evie brush past him, and he turned to follow the group. Along the second side of the aquarium, an elderly couple stood about ten feet away from the glass, and Noah walked toward them. He stopped no more than three feet away and stared at their profiles. The woman had wispy gray hair and the man had a bald head speckled with age spots. Both wore thick glasses and jackets two months ahead of the season. After a few seconds, the man raised an almost-steady finger at a penguin speeding past, and the woman giggled and clapped her hands twice without making any sound. He turned to his wife and leaned in for a quick kiss on her cheek.

Noah suddenly realized how weird it felt to be watching them. He was seeing the couple as they saw each other, without the world around. He had invaded a private moment. Being a Specter was more than being a ghost—it was being a spy.

With a rush of shame, Noah looked away. It wasn't right to be watching people, not without their awareness. He focused on an overweight penguin as it waddled to the end of the channel, splashed into the water, and torpedoed away, its flat flippers stroking at its sides.

After a few seconds, one of the scouts tapped his shoulder and Noah walked off.

In another private corner, Evie whispered, "Nice. Two more left. Go."

In the third room, a family of six stood near the aquarium, their attention on the underwater parade of penguins. The four children were about two years apart, the youngest a toddler with a blue pacifier between his lips. He was sitting up in a stroller, grunting his excitement.

Cabinets with items and information about penguins were on display throughout this room. Noah weaved between them. Once he was several feet past the last cabinet, a low ripping sound came from behind him, and his muscles clenched. The noise had been unmistakable. A zipper.

When he glanced back, the corner of a display cabinet glinted, and when Noah focused there, he saw a zipper—the rectangular pull tab and a few inches of metal teeth and surrounding cloth. One of the scouts must have snagged a portal pocket on the cabinet.

He saw that the entire family was looking that way. Even the toddler was leaning to one side of the stroller. The woman suddenly pressed her fingers to her cheeks and screamed.

Noah looked back again to see dozens of chameleons climbing over the display cabinet, ghosting it. Dozens more were pouring out of nowhere down toward the floor. He realized the portal pocket was open. The chameleons would keep coming and coming until it was closed.

Behind Noah, someone else shrieked. It sounded like the young girl, but given what was happening, it could very well have been the father.

The scout, whoever it was, managed to pull away from

the cabinet but then tripped—Noah could tell by how the chameleons fell. The pull tab of the zipper was now hanging by itself from the cabinet, which meant it had broken, leaving the portal wide open.

Two more screams came from the family as hundreds of chameleons were flooding the room. They began to crawl up the other display cabinets and along ridges in the wall of the building. As they climbed along the edges of the aquarium, part of the foggy glass seemed to disappear. Penguins stood by with their beady black eyes fixed on all the strange spectacles.

Noah turned to the family again. The older three children looked ready to faint. The toddler merely looked around, uninterested.

Someone hollered, "What are you *doing*?" to the scout on the floor, and Noah realized it had been Evie, still standing invisible at the back of the room. "Your pocket—close it!"

"I can't! It's broken!" came a voice from the ground—Richie's.

"Just hold it shut then!"

The chameleons stopped coming, and Noah realized Richie had managed to seal the portal.

But how badly had they compromised the Secret Zoo?

The mother gasped, "That . . . was . . . *hilarious*!"

Noah pulled down his eyebrows and stood very still.

"Hilarious?" one of the Specters said. "Try *pathetic*."

Noah was so confused that he became suddenly sure that he'd gone crazy—that the madness of the moment had melted his brain. The parents and the three older children started laughing. Only the toddler still seemed unamused.

"That was freaking *awesome*!" one of the older children said. "Did you see the looks on the penguins!"

"Yeah . . ." one of the Specters groaned. "Awesome, all right." After a brief pause, she added, "Girls, let's clean this mess up."

From the back of the room came the sound of zippers opening, one after another. Evie made a clicking sound with her tongue, and then the walls and floor blurred with movement as chameleons hurried for the open portals. As the chameleons on the scouts climbed down, the four friends became visible again. Richie was stretched out on his back. He was so perfectly still that he looked like someone who had died while making a snow angel. Noah realized that he'd crammed his hat into the top of his portal pocket to close it.

"Richie!" Ella said. "You okay?"

Richie continued to lie there, chameleons charging across his body.

The oldest kid in the family, a boy with a dimpled chin and a bad crew cut, brushed past Noah and maneuvered up to Richie, careful to step in the open spots between the chameleons. He leaned over and broke out laughing.

Ella pointed her thumb toward the boy and said to the Specters, "I'm guessing this corn dog and the rest of his"—she made quotation marks with her fingers—"*family* aren't from our neighborhood."

Out of their camouflage, the Specters walked toward the scouts, chameleons still clambering up their legs and squirming into their pockets. "Secret Cityzens," Evie said. "All the people are. A guard closed Penguin Palace as soon as we stepped in. We played it safe—and I'm glad we did."

The boy with the crew cut was still laughing.

"Why don't you make like a tree," Ella said to him.

The boy looked over to Ella, and through his laughter, said, "And leave?"

Ella crossed her arms and lifted her eyebrows. "No—find a *sawmill*."

The boy stopped laughing and his smile went flat. He hurried back over to his parents—or at least the people posing as them.

Ella grabbed Richie's jacket and hoisted him to his feet. Chameleons slid down his front and peppered the floor. She corrected his wardrobe with a tug here, a pull there. Then she grabbed the sides of his head and forced his gaze onto hers. "You okay?"

Richie nodded.

Once the last of the chameleons had portaled through the Specters' pockets, Jordynn walked over to the display cabinet and worked the pull tab of the broken zipper free. Then she offered it to Richie. "You'll want to fix this."

"Thanks," Richie said. He plucked his hat free and then slipped the tab into his pocket. Then he remembered the portal and reached in after the zipper piece.

Evie screamed, *"Richie—NO!"*

Richie pulled back his arm and flung as many as a dozen chameleons into the air. As they landed, they took off in different directions. He held his hand in front of his face. His fingers looked like pieces of chalk.

Evie jumped a few steps forward, saying, "You okay?"

Color seeped upward into Richie's flesh. Within seconds, he was back to normal.

"What happened?" Megan asked.

Evie said, "His hand—it portaled."

"I could feel it!" Richie said. "On the other side of the portal—I could feel my hand! Chameleons—they were crawling all over it!"

"You sure you're okay?"

Richie practiced bending his knuckles and turning his wrist. "I . . . I think so." His gaze settled on his wrist. "My watch! It's gone!"

"The chameleons. They stripped it off."

"But . . . it was my favorite one!"

Ella said, "That plastic watch with Boba Fett on it? Seriously? Didn't you get that thing from a gumball machine?"

This seemed to irritate Richie. As he forced his hat back on, he said, "No—I get *gumballs* from a gumball machine."

"Guys," Evie said, "you *can't* break your zippers. And you can never, *ever* reach into the portals."

"So where did his hand *go*?" Ella said. "The Secret Zoo, I get that. But where in the Secret Zoo?"

Evie frowned. "You really want to know?"

Everyone nodded but Richie, who was doing just the opposite, his bushy pom-pom wobbling around.

"Okay," Evie said. "I'll show you. Tomorrow."

❧ CHAPTER 10 ❧

SPIDERS, MAN

In the early evening after their first training with the Specters, Noah found himself home alone. His mom and dad had gone over to Richie's parents' house to swap stories and desserts, and Megan was over at Ella's. Noah did some schoolwork, goofed around on the Wii, and raided the fridge a few times. Around six-thirty, he headed upstairs for a warmer shirt.

In his closet, he was searching for his favorite sweatshirt when he noticed something moving on a pair of jeans: a plump spider, which quickly scurried out of sight.

"Disgusting."

He snatched up a slipper and held it like a club. As he reached out for his clothes, something threadlike fell across his fingers, and light shimmered on a silvery strand of web. He wiped his hand on his hip, reached out a second time, and slid about five sweatshirts over to one side. A spider appeared, clinging to the wall, perfectly still.

He eased the slipper forward a few inches. The spider kept motionless on the wall, its spindly legs making it look like an asterisk on a blank sheet of paper. As the shadow of the slipper fell onto it, the spider twitched and crawled forward an inch.

"Hold . . . still," Noah breathed.

As he prepared to deliver a blow, he felt something moving on the arm that was holding back his clothes. Then something else . . . and something else. When he looked and saw more than a dozen spiders crawling on him, he dropped his slipper and started swatting his arm. Some spiders fell to the ground and others had their black guts smeared across his sleeve. He stamped to squash the ones that were scrambling away, but he couldn't get them all—a few managed to crawl up the wall and escape into the heat vent.

Noah's eyes widened. The spiders had come from the ductwork in the walls.

He dropped to his hands and knees in front of the vent and pressed an ear to the metal slats. From deep inside came a low groan, and then cool air brushed his cheek. When he saw that two screws secured the vent cover to the wall, he jumped up and rushed out of the closet. In the garage, he snatched a small flashlight and screwdriver from his father's toolbox. Back in his closet, he went to work removing the screws. The vent cover dropped to the floor with a flat clang, and a rectangular hole stared at Noah like a single black eye in the face of the wall. He shined the flashlight inside, revealing the steel duct, which made an immediate right turn for the basement.

He eased himself forward. With his face and the flashlight just inches from the open vent, he stopped. Would the duct be full of spiders? Was the magic of the Secret Zoo—the magic he'd seen in the cellar of Clarksville Elementary and in the pockets of the Specters—involved here? Was DeGraff behind this? Or was so much going on in Noah's life that his imagination was overwhelming him?

He worked up his courage and stared into the hole, aiming his flashlight into the depths to reveal what there was to be seen. Nothing. There was no mold, and Noah couldn't even locate the spiders that had crawled away.

A familiar click from far below revealed how the furnace was ramping up to heat the house again. A soft, cool wind began to tousle his hair; seconds later, the wind turned warm.

Noah pulled back his head and sat wondering about the spiders.

He screwed the vent cover back on, stood, checked his clothes on the rack for more spiders, found a few, and then squashed them. On his way downstairs to return his father's tools, he made a mental note to discuss with the scouts all the weirdness he'd been experiencing in his closet. Maybe they'd have an idea about what was going on.

◄⊙ CHAPTER 11 ⊙►

THE STREETS OF TRANSPARENCY

"No . . . way," Richie said.

The scouts were on the Streets of Transparency. Just inside the portal, they'd halted so suddenly that the rubbery soles of Richie's running shoes had squeaked and Ella had bumped into Richie's back.

"No . . . way," Richie said again in a perfect echo.

The scouts were on a bumpy cobblestone street that was little more than a narrow alley. On both sides rose walls with intricate stonework, weighty wood doors, and windows with no glass. Short bridges reached across the alley, and beneath canvas awnings, iron railings boxed in balconies.

Parts of the alley were covered with thousands of colorful chameleons, and other parts were . . . gone. Or seemed to be, anyway. Street signs hovered in the air; tree branches didn't have any trunks; the corners of buildings and doorways were chipped away; colorful awnings and iron balcony rails were full of holes—holes that seemed to be moving.

"Uhhh . . ." Ella said, tipping her head so her ponytail dangled down her back. "I'm thinking . . . *weird.*"

Noah said, "The chameleons . . . they're doing this, right?"

"Of course," Evie said. "Camouflaging—it's just what chameleons do. Sometimes they even mirage."

"Mirage?" Noah said, remembering that Mr. Darby had mentioned this. "What's that?"

"It's an advanced Specter move," Evie said. Then she glanced over at her friends. "Should I show them?"

The other Specters stayed quiet. Finally, Lee-Lee shrugged to show she didn't care.

Evie opened one pocket and a line of chameleons streamed out and spread across her body. Strips of her faded away and then came back into focus looking different. Her skin tone lightened. Her shoulders and hips seemed to narrow, and she shrank a few inches. Eyeglasses appeared on her face, and her long bangs now seemed tucked up under the broad, ribbed cuff of a red winter cap. Evie wasn't Evie anymore. She was Richie.

The real Richie gasped.

"No *way!*" Ella said. "How . . ." Her lips moved into different shapes, producing no sound.

The Richie that was Evie smiled. "Like I said, it's an advanced move." Evie's voice was her own. "Comes from years of practice—of being so close to the chameleons. We think, they do. We imagine—they create."

Richie took a cautious step forward. He touched Evie's arm, shoulder, head. He peeled back one side of her open jacket and saw his pocket of nerd-gear. Then he took a step back and looked into his own jacket. "They're not the same," he said. "You're missing some things."

"Miraging works that way. I created the image from my memory. It's not like I pay attention to that stuff you carry around."

Ella said, "Man! When do we learn to do *that!*"

"You don't," Evie said. "We barely have enough time to teach you how to ghost. And so far you're not real good at that."

The real Richie still looked ready to faint, and his eyes kept shifting in their sockets. "I can't . . ." His voice trailed off and his expression changed with a new thought. "Oh my . . . Am I really *that* skinny?"

Ella laughed. "Turn sideways, Evie. Show him." When Evie did, Ella added, "See? You almost disappear, wafer-boy."

Richie's jaw dropped down a few inches. "But my butt . . ."

"Yeah . . ." Ella said. "Practically inverted, we know."

The mirage of Richie began to break up as ghostly shapes moved across it—the chameleons. Seconds later, the mirage was gone, and Evie stood in its place, looking like her normal self again.

"Come on," Evie said. "Something you should see."

"What?"

"The Portal Place. It used to be an old bakery. That should give you an idea of why you never want to do what Richie did yesterday in Penguin Palace."

As the scouts followed the Specters down the street, Megan said, "Can your portals go anywhere with you? Even beyond the Clarksville Zoo?"

Evie nodded but kept quiet as she led them up a steep flight of stairs and then onto a new street. As Noah's heels twisted and turned on the bumpy cobblestone, he took in the new-but-familiar sights: arched bridges, dark doorways, glassless windows. He watched as parts of the city seemed to fade away: railings, signs, the peaks of rooftops. Other parts reappeared. Chameleons were crawling in all directions, thousands of tiny eyes staring down on the scouts.

At last, Evie said, "Bhanu didn't create our portals. We did."

"The Specters?"

Evie shook her head. "The Secret Society. A team of magical scientists."

The scouts kept quiet and waited for more as the group continued down the street.

"They were geniuses, and like a lot of geniuses, they didn't fit in with anyone, so they usually worked by themselves. Somehow they redeveloped Bhanu's magic and created a velvet curtain—a single portal—which could cross beyond the boundaries of the Clarksville Zoo. But before they could share their findings, they went amiss."

The scouts knew what this meant. In rare cases, some portals could misfire and cause people and animals to disappear into unknown places.

"Their curtain was stripped down and sent to the lab of the other magical scientists, who studied it for years but could never figure out what made it so powerful. When it was decided to lock the curtain in a secure place, the Descenders petitioned Council for the right to use it. They were granted permission to use half of the curtain—the Secret Council keeping the other half in case of future studies—and the Specters were born."

"So the Specters *are* part of the Descenders," Megan said. "It doesn't seem that way."

Evie glanced at Jordynn, who shook her head so suddenly that waves moved through her bushy hair.

"That's a story for another day," Evie said. "If ever."

Noah grunted. Another secret of the Secret Zoo that the scouts weren't trusted enough to know.

Noah said, "DeGraff—he found a way to portal beyond the Clarksville Zoo. You think his magic is as strong as yours?"

Evie and the other Specters stopped walking and turned to a small shop where an open door separated two bay windows. Bright chameleons spotted the door frame and panes of glass, and a near-invisible sign beneath a near-invisible awing read, " i y r at nd Se o   e t s."

"City Treats and Sector Sweets," Evie read, filling in the letters the chameleons had camouflaged. "The Portal Place is inside."

"Evie—what about DeGraff?" Noah said.

Evie tipped her head to one side and allowed her bangs to slip across her face. "Kid—he's only getting started."

Before Noah could respond, she tiptoed through the chameleons on the porch and passed through the open door of City Treats and Sector Sweets. Glass display cabinets ran along three of the walls. Once upon a time they'd undoubtedly been filled with donuts and muffins. Now they had mounds of chameleons. The colorful lizards also covered the counters, the ovens, the registers.

Noah looked over the Specters: Kaleena's long braids; Jordynn's wild tuft of hair; Lee-Lee's long, curling eyebrows. They were stepping into open spots on the floor, careful not to squash any chameleons beneath their black boots and bright hiking shoes.

Noah saw that his legs, from the knees down, had turned invisible. Same with the other scouts and Specters. The chameleons were running across their feet.

A chameleon fell off an overhead chandelier, landed on Ella's head, and got tangled in her ponytail. As she tried to yank it away, she accidentally tore off its tail. She shrieked and violently shook her head, flinging what was left of the reptile across the room. When she spotted Richie laughing, she tossed the severed tail at him.

"Real funny!" she said.

"It was just its tail!" Richie chuckled. "It's not like you killed it!"

"I'm not worried about the chameleon—I'm worried about *me*!" She reached up and combed her fingers through her ponytail. "So *gross*—I probably have invisible guts in my hair!"

Evie led the group into the back of the store. After all the spectacles of the Secret Zoo—the flowering abyss of the Forest of Flight, the snowy tundra of Arctic Town, the slides and waterfalls of the Wotter Park—the simplicity of the Portal Place was a bit surprising. The ordinary room, packed with chameleons, held two steel storage racks. From each rack hung twelve canvas packs arranged in pairs; brown and plain, they looked a lot like potato sacks.

"This is it?" Richie asked.

"What did you expect from an old donut shop?"

Chameleons crowded the racks, their feet curled around the steel rods. Thousands of independent eyes looked off in all directions.

Evie said, "Now you understand why it's important to close your portals."

"What are they doing?" Megan asked.

"Waiting," Evie answered.

"For what?"

"For this."

Evie reached down and unzipped her left pants pocket. From a bag on the storage rack came the unmistakable sound of a zipper—dozens of metal teeth pulling apart, a sound clearly amplified by the magic in Evie's pocket. A small cluster of chameleons jumped to attention and slipped into the pack, then immediately appeared on Evie, a line of twenty scurrying up her leg. They spread out, camouflaging her. Evie's left pocket closed and the right opened. As the chameleons retreated into it and appeared back on the rack, Evie slowly became visible, her hands on her hips.

"Try it," Evie said. "Get a feel for how quickly the chameleons respond."

The scouts glanced at one another, a bit uncertain,

then opened their left pockets. They began to practice portaling chameleons from the storage rack to their bodies, drifting in and out of visibility. After a few minutes, Richie pointed across the room and said, "Look! Boba Fett!"

"Can't be," Ella said. "He bit the dust in episode five, remember?"

"My watch!"

It was wrapped around the body of a large, blue chameleon, which had apparently wriggled its way into the plastic band.

"That belongs to me!" Richie said. He began to walk toward it but stopped when the chameleon and the watch disappeared.

"Forget it," Evie said as she stared out at the writhing mass. "It's not worth the trouble—believe me."

Richie continued to gaze at the spot where his watch had been. "First my shoes . . ." he said, referring to how an ape had stripped off his running shoes on his first time in the City of Species, "and now this! I'm going to end up without any clothes!"

"Yikes!" Ella said. "Let's just hope you're invisible when it happens."

Evie motioned for the door. "C'mon, we need to get back to the Clarksville Zoo. You got another chance to get this right. And this time, there won't be any actors."

CHAPTER 12

SNICKERS SNATCHERS

"Where we going?" Ella asked once the scouts and Specters had portaled back to the Clarksville Zoo.

"PizZOOria. You guys up for a snack?"

"As always," Richie said. "And, as always, no cash. Can someone float me a few bucks?"

A few of the Specters chuckled.

"You're not going to need to pay," Sara said. "When you're ghosted, everything's free."

"But . . . that's stealing," Megan said.

Sara made a strange sound—part laugh, part grunt. "For you . . . it's practice."

"I don't know . . ." Richie said in his usual trembling voice. "There are rules for—"

"Rules don't apply to ghosts."

Noah felt a surge of excitement. Hadn't some buried-deep piece of him always wanted to shrug away the endless restrictions kept on him? No fussing, no back talk, no texting at the table, no phone calls after ten o'clock. Noah wasn't even permitted to choose his bedtime. The Specters—they seemed to answer only to themselves.

They merged onto the sidewalk and headed through Arctic Town. Noah thought of Blizzard again, and he wondered if it would be okay to steal if it was part of an attempt to rescue his friend.

They soon came upon PizZOOria, the largest restaurant in the zoo, and waited at the front entrance. When two kids with wet globs of cotton candy stuck to their cheeks pushed their way out of the building, the Crossers, one after the other, eased through the doors before they closed.

The restaurant had a decent crowd for such a cold fall weekday. Five groups of people sat munching pizza, hot dogs, and corn chips. Cups of hot chocolate steamed, and jackets were draped across empty tabletops. The long front counter curved to follow the shape of the building. Behind it, hot pretzels warmed in glass cabinets and popcorn poppers popped. The air smelled like cheeseburgers and chocolate, and it seemed to have a weight, as if permanently saturated by the grease from all the years.

Noah felt a tug on his arm and moved in that direction until he bumped into someone. In one corner of PizZOOria, the Specters and scouts huddled.

"Go get your snack . . ." Lee-Lee whispered.

"You first," Ella whispered back.

"We already went," Lee-Lee said. She crunched a potato chip.

"How?" Ella said. Her voice was somewhere to Noah's left. "We just walked in, for crying out loud!"

"Not hardly," Lee-Lee said. "We've been here at least a full minute."

Ella said, "I guess you girls get extra points for being speedy."

Lee-Lee crunched another chip.

"Go," Sara said to the scouts. "And don't get caught."

One of the scouts bumped Noah, who realized it was Ella when her fuzzy earmuff touched his cheek. Then, as either Richie or Megan bumped his other side, Noah felt the patter and prick of clawed feet as a few chameleons moved to new spots on his body.

He scanned the long, silvery curve of the countertop and studied the snacks stacked upon it. Bags of pretzels, chips, and caramel corn. M&M's and Milky Ways and

3 Musketeers. Pumpkin seeds, sunflower seeds, bubble gum, breath mints.

About thirty feet away, wire shelves were attached to the half wall of the counter, candy bars stocked on them. It would be almost no effort to ease up to them and slip a candy bar into one of his pockets.

Noah rounded an empty table, stepped around a garbage bin, then ducked beneath a wooden rail. Several feet in front of him, the candy rack waited. He took a few more steps and turned his hip toward a neat pile of Kit Kats. As he reached for one, his hand halted. He knew it wasn't right to steal—he'd been taught that all his life—and now something inside him was trying to keep the candy bar out of his pocket.

But for some reason it felt good to be doing something wrong. It seemed like he was about to punch through a wall of rules—something built brick by brick by the people he loved.

A restaurant worker suddenly appeared beyond the counter, less than two feet in front of him. A teenage boy, he had bad hair, a splattering of red pimples, and a wisp of whiskers on his chin. A name tag reading, "Hello! My name is Derik!!!!" was pinned crookedly to his shirt. He was chewing bubble gum, his lips smacking wetly. When he let a silent burp escape his mouth, Noah turned his face away.

Noah stood perfectly still, his invisible hand hovering above the Kit Kats. He and the teenager, Derik, were now practically nose to nose. Beside them on the counter sat a pretzel warmer—a steamy glass cabinet with wire racks and a little door. Derik grabbed a napkin, reached into the cabinet, and plucked a pretzel from a steel bar. Noah took in a breath of fragrant, humid air from the cabinet, and stifled a sneeze. But Derik heard the sound and shifted his eyes directly toward him. Then he squinted.

Noah held his breath and became aware of his beating heart. His dangling fingers began to tremble. Should he turn and run? Maybe he could slip out of PizZOOria before anyone else could mark him?

Another restaurant worker, a boy with scraggly brown hair, walked behind Derik and playfully bumped into him, saying, "Don't be checking out the ladies, man."

Derik's cheeks flushed, and he quickly crammed the pretzel into a bag and walked off to the registers. Noah let out a quiet gush of air and felt his shoulders slump. He looked behind him to see what Derik had been staring at: a curvy teenage girl with flowing blond hair.

Noah grabbed a Kit Kat, slipped it into his jacket pocket, and ducked beneath the rail. He hurried back over to the Specters, his careful footsteps soundless on the floor.

"Who is that?" one of the Specters whispered.

"Noah."

"You get something?"

Noah nodded and then remembered no one could see him. "Yeah. Kit Kat."

Ella and Megan shared what they'd taken: a Twix and a pack of bubble gum, respectively. Just when Noah was about to ask where Richie was, Ella said, "You've got to be kidding," and he realized a bunch of customers were curiously looking around. There was nothing to see, but Noah heard a *tick! tick! tick! tick!*—like pebbles bouncing in a box. The noise drew closer and louder and then stopped altogether. Richie.

"Let me guess . . ." Ella whispered to Richie. "Tic Tacs?"

"They had Cherry Passion," Richie said. "My fave."

"Okay . . ." Ella said below the noise of the restaurant. "There are two things wrong with this. One . . . Tic Tacs are for grandmas. And two . . . they're noisy. Kids trying to be inconspicuous should *not* put them in their pockets."

"Wow," Richie said. "Inconspicuous . . . a five-syllable word. Nice work, El."

"All right, enough," Sara said to Ella and Richie. "C'mon—let's get out of here."

Someone brushed past Noah and he headed to the exit, where the Crossers followed a mother and her two children out the door.

"See the trees over there?" Evie asked. "Go."

As they headed that way, Noah whispered, "How's that bubble gum?" to his sister. When she didn't answer, he said, "Meg?" a bit louder than he should have.

No response. Noah looked over his shoulder just in time to see one of the restaurant doors crack open a foot and quickly close, as if someone had slipped out. But no one was there.

Noah thought he heard footsteps, and then he sensed someone standing beside him.

"Meg?"

"Yeah?" Noah realized she was out of breath.

"How's the gum?"

"Oh . . . not bad, I guess."

It was obvious that she was lying. His sister wasn't chewing gum. She'd slipped back into the restaurant to return what she had taken.

"We got one more stop," Evie said. "Back in the Secret Zoo. Follow me."

As Noah headed off following Evie's marks—a shake of a branch, a step in the snow—guilt struck him again. He turned his attention to the invisible candy bar in his hand, its weight and shape. Maybe he should return his too. It wouldn't take long to run back into PizZOOria. The Specters wouldn't even need to know.

Instead, he tore open the wrapper and bit down, never remembering a time when chocolate had tasted so sweet.

CHAPTER 13

THE FEATHER, THE QUILL, THE HAIR FROM A MANE

"You got to be joking," Richie said.

"Nope," said Evie. "Dead serious. It's a great test."

Evie had led the scouts to Tarsier Terrace, a winding balcony attached to a building in the City of Species. In the nearby trees, thousands of tarsiers went about their business of training for perimeter patrol, a nightly surveillance of the Clarksville Zoo. The Specters were sitting at one of the many tables across the terrace, sipping drinks, their legs kicked up in various ways: on the table-top, ankles crossed; over the arms of chairs, knees bent; on the terrace railing, heels against the stone.

Evie's cheeks sank into her face as she sucked from a straw. Then she said to the scouts, "Look—just ghost up and go out into the city. You need to bring back three things from the Descenders on post at the city gateways without being noticed. A red feather . . . a quill . . . and a hair from a mane."

"Do they know about this?" Ella asked. "The Descenders?"

Evie shook her head. "What would be the point then?"

"What if they catch us?"

Evie shrugged.

A tarsier jumped down from an overhead branch, landing on the tabletop. It tried to sniff the bow in Lee-Lee's shoelace, perhaps thinking it was a bug, but the Specter shooed it away with a not-so-gentle thrust of her foot.

Without a word, Noah opened his left portal pocket, inviting the chameleons to crawl out and camouflage him.

"Okay," Ella said. "I guess we're doing this." As she unzipped her pocket, so did Richie and Megan. Chameleons scattered across them, and within seconds, they were out of sight.

"Let's go," Noah said.

"A red feather, a quill, and a hair from a mane," Evie reminded as the scouts walked off. "You got thirty minutes."

The four friends walked down a winding staircase and stepped out onto the streets of the City of Species.

Overhead, birds skipped across branches and sunlight streamed through open places in the colorful canopy of leaves. Hummingbirds darted from spot to spot, their tireless wings whirring. Sprays of water rose stories above the stone fountains set in the streets.

"Okay," Megan said, "where do we start?"

Noah turned to look at his sister, forgetting she was invisible. "Pick a sector," he said to what seemed an empty space beside him. "Every city gateway is guarded by a Descender."

"Whoa!" Ella said. "That elephant almost flattened me!"

Noah glanced back for a close view of a wide gray rump, tail wagging. "I totally forgot the animals can't see us," he said. "Don't get squashed."

The scouts rounded a bend in the road, careful to side-step a trotting rhino, and came upon the Secret Penguin Palace, a massive building with bricks the size of pyramid stones. The weighty eaves of its roof rested on marble columns that were sculptured to look like tall blocks of ice. Its entrance, a single velvet curtain, was being guarded by a Descender.

"C'mon," Noah said. "Let's get close."

He eased his way toward the building, confident that his friends were in tow. He stopped about twenty feet from the entrance. The guard, a boy in his late teens with a sparse, wiry beard, wore a leather jacket with a series of curved blades on the outsides of his sleeves. Noah nudged his friends and headed back out into the street. When they were a safe distance away, he said, "Let's check another one."

They passed coffee shops and grocery stores. Noah sometimes forgot that the City of Species was full of people who worked and shopped and went to school and did other everyday things—just alongside animals.

Another sector came into view—the Secret Butterfly Nets. The glass building was so tall and narrow that the butterflies inside seemed to be shooting toward the sky like a volcanic eruption. At the sector's portal, a guard stood by. His clothes contained animal armor in strategic spots: elbows, knees, shoulders. Because he wasn't wearing feathers, quills, or a mane, the scouts quietly circled back into the city streets.

As Noah led the way, he marked his location with his voice: "I'm here." "Over here." "I'm here." "It's me." They stepped over several sloths and dodged a peacock's tail feathers. They splashed through narrow streams and squinted through the drifting mist of waterfalls.

At the Secret Giraffic Jam, the scouts inched up to the velvet gateway, where a girl Descender was dangling upside down from a branch by an artificial tail. When they were back out of earshot, Ella said, "How does she keep from fainting? The magic?"

Noah shrugged. Despite having crosstrained for a year, the scouts really hadn't learned much about the Descenders, the kin of those murdered in the Sasquatch Rebellion. The scouts knew the Descenders were part of the Secret Zoo's army, people who used magic to take on animal powers, but that was really all.

Noah glanced back and saw the girl dangling upside down again, and he wondered what it would be like to be a Descender. To fly with wings. To swing a tail. To slice through his problems with razor-sharp blades. To be so powerful.

When they reached the Secret Forest of Flight, a stadium-sized birdhouse with a giant domed roof, they discovered a guard who looked a lot like a porcupine, quills dangling off every part of his body.

"Check it out," Ella said, her voice coming from somewhere behind Noah. "Solana's twin."

"And he's got just what we need," Noah said. "I think only one of us should go. Who wants—"

"I'll do it," Megan said.

She brushed past Noah as she made her way to the guard. Noah waited and watched. The Descender looked left, then right, then coughed into his fist, causing quills to quiver. A few birds flew out from the curtain and soared past his head.

"Where is she?" Richie asked.

"Who knows . . ." Ella said.

But just then, all three of the scouts found out. A loose quill on the guard's shoulder rose into the air, where it quickly disappeared, undoubtedly in Megan's grasp. The Descender glanced at his shoulder, as if he'd felt something there, and then casually looked away.

"She got it!" Ella screamed under her breath. "Man— she rocks!"

Megan's voice came from beside them: "One down, two to go."

"*Girrrlll . . .*" Ella sang, "I'd high-five you right now if I wasn't afraid to miss and slap your face!"

"C'mon," Noah said. "Let's get the others."

He led them up the street with another chorus of "I'm here . . . Over here . . . I'm here . . . It's me." Beside a coffee stand, he was nearly plowed over by three men in green lab coats—magical scientists. The scouts turned down an alley and came out near the portal to the Little Dogs of the Prairie sector, where another Descender stood guard. A lionlike mane fell from the raised hood of his jacket across his shoulders and down his back.

"Number two," Noah said.

"Speaking of which," said Richie. "Remember that question I had about using the bathroom while we're ghosted?"

"Tell me you're joking. . . ." Ella said.

"I can't help it!" Richie explained. "All this sneaking around—you know I have a nervous stomach!"

"Dude—you're going to have to hold it," Noah said curtly. "Okay . . . I'll take this one."

He stepped away from his friends and eased across the street, ducking a snake coiled around a low tree branch. As he drew close to the portal, he saw how the Descender's furry gloves had bare, meaty pads on the palms. No doubt he could strike out with the strength of a lion, and Noah worried that he would if he felt Noah pulling his hair.

Noah stepped in between the back of the guard and the velvet curtain. As he stood gathering his courage, a line of prairie dogs trailed out from the portal, a few trampling over his invisible feet. Once the rambunctious rodents were out of sight, he reached out, pinched a thick hair in the Descender's mane, and then thought better of plucking it. He spotted a loose hair on the Descender's jacket and took that one instead. Then he tiptoed back to his friends, who responded to his "Where are you?" whispers.

"You get it?" Ella asked.

"Got it."

"Awesome. One more to go . . ."

"A red feather," Noah reminded them.

The scouts headed out again, navigating alleys and streets. They quickly came across Platypus Playground, where a frowning Descender stood, long red feathers trailing down his arms and back.

"Who wants to go?" Noah whispered. "Richie?"

Richie's answer came quick: "Nope."

"I'll do it," Ella volunteered.

Noah felt the air swirl as Ella moved past him. He fixed his eyes on the Descender and waited. A platypus walked out of the portal and ran between the Descender's legs, its flat bill looking like a giant shoehorn sweeping across the street. A minute passed, then another.

"What's taking her so long?" Megan whispered.

"I don't know. Maybe—"

Just then, a bright red feather floated off the ground near the guard's feet. A second later, it disappeared, and Ella quickly returned, humming the theme from *Mission Impossible* under her breath.

"You go, girl," Megan said.

"C'mon," Noah said. "Let's get back."

With all three items in their possession, the scouts turned and headed back toward Tarsier Terrace, Ella still humming, this time louder than before.

CHAPTER 14

TALKS ON THE TARSIER TERRACE

Back at Tarsier Terrace, Noah, Ella, and Megan dropped their spoils onto the table in front of the Specters. On their way across the city, the scouts had sent back their chameleons, and they were once again in plain view.

Evie swung her legs down and leaned over the table. She sniffed the hair, twirled the feather, and poked her palm with the point of the quill.

"They from Descenders?" Sara asked Evie.

Evie confirmed that they were with the slightest nod. To Noah, she seemed to be working hard to keep her expression flat.

"That's right," Ella said. "We sort of rock."

Evie allowed a small smile onto her face. "Nice."

From off to their side came the sound of clapping and a man's voice: "Indeed it was!"

Mr. Darby was walking toward the table with at least three tarsiers perched on his velvet jacket, their big cartoonish eyes staring out. One kept nipping at the old man's bushy beard. At his side was Solana, her long hair tucked behind her ears, her Descender gear retracted into her blue jacket and fingerless gloves.

"All items are accounted for?" Mr. Darby asked the Specters as he stepped up to the table.

Sara nodded, her tall Mohawk slicing through the air.

"Excellent! And in how much time?"

Noah checked his watch. "Twenty-three minutes."

Mr. Darby smiled. "Well done, my young Crossers! I'm here to inform you all that Council is finalizing a time for our rescues. I expect to hear from Marlo soon, and I'll be able to send the scouts home with this information if they can afford the time." He looked expectantly at Noah, who quickly checked with his friends and then nodded. "Excellent!" As Mr. Darby stretched his arm to pat Richie's shoulder, a tarsier on his shoulder fixed its gaze on the pom-pom on Richie's cap.

"Don't even think about it!" Richie warned the animal, referring to the scouts' first visit to the terrace when a tarsier had attacked Richie's pom-pom, thinking it was a bug.

The tarsier blinked its big eyes and scrambled to a new spot on Mr. Darby's jacket.

Mr. Darby said, "Should we have a bite to eat until our kingfisher friend arrives?"

The Specters at the table moved their legs and scooted closer to one another, and the other Specters took seats, leaving only one open spot. As Richie pulled back the chair to sit down, Ella slid into it before he could.

"Wha—! How rude!" Richie said.

"The rude dude gets the food," Ella said, making Lee-Lee and Elakshi chuckle.

Off to one side was a pair of smaller tables. Megan and Mr. Darby settled in at one, and Noah and Solana sat down at the other, leaving Richie the only person standing.

"Where am I supposed to sit?" Richie asked as he looked around.

"You snooze, you lose," Ella said.

"Dr. Seuss—would you quit with the rhymes already!" Richie shot back. His gaze came to rest on something. "Hey! Look who it is!"

Noah saw Zak sitting alone at a table for two against one edge of the terrace, his fingers probing through the electronics inside an open box.

"See you guys!" Richie said as he hurried off toward the person he undoubtedly was most interested in.

"You try one of these?" Solana asked. She was holding up a small ball of chocolate between her thumb and forefinger.

"What is it?" Noah asked.

Solana shrugged. "Chocolate-covered something."

Noah reached into one of the bags that the waiter had brought to their table, plucked out a single chocolate, and popped it into his mouth, where it melted onto his tongue.

"Wow!" Noah said, careful to wipe a drip from his lower lip.

As Solana bit into another chocolate, she gazed off toward the trees. Noah followed her stare and saw nothing interesting. He took a closer look at Solana and saw the emptiness in her eyes.

"You're worried," he pointed out.

"Huh?"

"The Descenders—you're worried."

"Oh," Solana said. And then she gazed back at the same spot, as if she'd abandoned something there. "Yeah."

"That's okay," Noah said. "I am, too. We all are."

"I just . . . I've known them all my life."

"And you'll *continue* to know them. We'll get them back."

Solana looked back at him. "Are you worried about Saturday?"

"A little." Then Noah corrected his lie. "A lot." He bit down on a new chocolate, caramel bursting onto his tongue.

Solana went to bite into another piece of candy and stopped. She turned the chocolate in her fingers and then dropped it onto the table. "I wonder if they're eating."

It took a few seconds for Noah to realize she was still talking about her friends.

"DeGraff . . ." she said, "that maniac—I doubt he's even feeding them."

Noah wanted to say something to ease her fears, but everything he could think of felt like a lie. He settled on the one thing he was certain of. "Your friends are tough."

Solana stared at the table. "They need to eat. They need water."

"It's only been a few days," Noah reminded her. "People can go days without food."

Solana frowned. Then she picked up her chocolate from the table and put it back into the bowl.

"The way he took them," Solana said, softly shaking her head. "In that cellar . . . he just dragged them off, in and out of the shadows."

Noah nodded. "Scariest thing I've ever seen."

"Like they were *nothing*," Solana said. "Not people, anyway."

Noah nodded again.

A few minutes passed in silence. Noah reached for another chocolate and decided against it. At another table, someone laughed, and Solana and Noah turned to see a smile on Evie's face.

Solana said, "The Specters—they seem to like you guys. That's saying something."

"Haven't you noticed why?" Noah asked. "It's Ella."

Solana turned back to the Specters. Their attention was fixed on Ella, who was telling a story with theatrical gestures.

Ella banged her fist against the table and the Specters jumped in their chairs. Startled by the noise, a few tarsiers on the overhead branches took off to new spots, their hind legs kicking like kangaroos'.

Solana said, "She's always so . . . so . . . I don't know . . ."

"Sassy?"

"Yeah . . . sassy. Has she always been that way?"

Noah shrugged. "Yes and no. She changed when she lost her dad."

"He died?"

"Worse. He left the house and never came back."

Solana stared at Ella. "Yeah, well, the Specters know a thing or two about loss, that's for sure."

"So do you guys," Noah said. "The Descenders, I mean." He was thinking about the family members the

Descenders had lost during the Sasquatch Rebellion. "What's going on between you—the Specters and Descenders, I mean. How come—"

Solana interrupted by sliding a bowl of popcorn over to him. "Did you try this?"

Noah thought to press the issue, then decided against it. He reached into the bowl, grabbed a small wad of popcorn, and stuffed it into his mouth. On his tongue, a dozen flavors erupted—salt and sugar and honey. Guilt washed over him as he thought of Tank and the captured Descenders, and he wished the tastes would go away.

"Solana . . ." Noah said.

"Yeah?" Solana asked.

"Was it your great-grandparents that were . . . you know . . ."

"Murdered?"

Noah nodded.

"*Great*-great-grandparents," Solana answered. "My great-grandparents were kids when it happened."

"Were your great-grandparents Descenders?" Noah asked.

"Some of the first," Solana answered. "And some of the best. Their anger—it was pure. Their need for revenge . . . it completely drove them."

Noah wondered if this was a good thing, but he stayed quiet.

"We're a few generations out now," Solana said. "That type of anger . . . time dilutes it."

"But you . . . you still feel it?"

"We *cling* to it. It's a part of our tradition—of what it means to be a Descender. It's who we are."

As Solana used her hand to flip her hair off her shoulder, Noah noticed her glove. Black, shiny leather, it was held on by a wide Velcro strap, and a small velvet patch was stitched to it. Each sleeve stopped short of the first knuckle, leaving much of her fingers exposed. Looking at the glove now, Noah could hardly believe that fifteen-inch barbs could spring from the back of it like the claws of a comic book hero.

"What's it like?" Noah asked, suddenly unable to repress his curiosity.

"What's what like?"

"Being a Descender."

Solana took some time to answer, her gaze shifting to different spots across the terrace.

"The truth?" Solana asked.

Noah leaned forward in his chair and nodded.

"Awesome. Sometimes terrible and sometimes terrifying . . . but always awesome. There are times when I hate it, and times when I wouldn't trade it for anything in the world—yours or mine."

An unexpected feeling coursed through Noah, and

it took a few seconds for him to realize what it was. Envy. What it would be like to sprout quills, gloves, or wings? To crash through a wall with a tail attached to his spine? To jump twenty feet into the air? Then Noah had such a strong thought that it consumed all his others. If he were a Descender, what animal power would he take?

The conversation paused for more than a minute, and then, from nowhere, Solana said, "You know . . . I petitioned for you to go with Evie."

"Huh?"

"Council—I petitioned them. I asked if we could divide up you guys during the rescues—send your friends to the Waterford Zoo, and you to Creepy Critters."

"Wha—?" Noah glanced over at the table with the Specters. "Me? Why?"

"*Why?*" Solana asked. "C'mon—you really need to ask that?"

Noah was totally confused now.

"The Dark Lands—who rescued Megan? Who brought down the portal to the Secret Creepy Critters in Gator Falls? And who rescued me in your school? You bring something unique to the table. You're different—I don't know why. I think it's partly because you're an Outsider."

Noah had no idea what to say.

After some time, Solana continued, "Council—they're

idiots, sometimes. It's not a good idea—sending Specters to rescue Descenders."

Solana looked over at the Specter table and then back at Noah. "I'm not going to lie to you. I don't trust Evie's crew. Sometimes I worry . . ." Her voice trailed off, and when it came back, it was quieter than ever. "Sometimes I worry Evie will leave the Descenders in there. Deliberately. Sometimes I think she'll come out with Tank but see to it that the others don't make it."

"C'mon!" Noah said. "You don't seriously believe that, do you? I mean, Evie showed up at my school to help us, remember?"

"The Secret Zoo was at stake then. Now . . . now it's just a few Descenders."

Noah could hardly believe what he was hearing. Was Evie really capable of something so sinister? She was odd, certainly, but Solana was practically talking about murder.

"The Descenders want revenge," Solana said. "But the Specters . . . they want it even more."

"Against *who*?" Noah asked. And then the answer quickly became obvious. "Solana—what did you guys *do* to them?"

"Shhh!" Solana said. And she tipped her head to the side.

When Noah looked over, he saw Evie watching them.

Ella crunched a handful of mixed nuts and said, "Look . . . I know things are pretty horrible right now—DeGraff, the Descenders, Blizzard and Little Big—but you girls have this . . . *power*, and I sense you've never done anything fun with it. Am I right?"

The six girls traded glances with one another. Then Evie turned back to Ella. "Fun?"

"Fun," Ella said. She looked off into the treetops and then leaned forward, her ponytail sweeping over her shoulder and dangling above the chocolates. "Here, watch this." Smiling, she walked over to a place behind Kaleena, stood on her tiptoes, and snatched a tarsier from a low branch. The puny animal turned its head back and forth, its big eyes full of fright. "Easy, little guy," Ella said. "I'm not going to hurt you—we're just going to have a little fun."

She peered over her shoulders to make sure no one was paying attention to her, then opened a zipper on her cargo pants. Chameleons spread along her body, camouflaging both her and the animal.

"Watch and learn, ladies," she said.

One of the Specters giggled as Ella, invisible, headed off with the tarsier carefully cupped in her hands. She walked past a table with two magical scientists, old men with gray mustaches and green lab coats. Then she passed two women sharing a chocolate dessert. At another table, a young girl was reading a book while a young lemur slept on her lap. None of them had any idea that Ella had walked beside them.

At Richie and Zak's table, she moved in behind her friend. The two boys were investigating a small, three-pronged piece of steel on the table, probing both ends with their fingertips, as if it were a maybe-dead bug. Zak called it a ceramic resonator, which, to Ella, sounded like something her mother might cook a pot roast in.

She raised her hands above Richie and very carefully opened her fingers. The sticky pads of the tarsier's toes popped free from her skin, then the animal plopped down on Richie's head, where it immediately came out of its camouflage, its round eyes bulging out more than ever. It spotted the poofy pom-pom on Richie's cap and lunged upon it, biting into its strands of yarn.

Ella stepped away just in time to avoid her friend as he jumped up from the table. As he reached for his cap, his fingertips grazed the tarsier and he shrieked. Across the length of the winding terrace, heads turned.

Richie knocked his chair over and moved into the aisle. As Ella made her way back to the table, he screamed, "ERRR!" and "E-RAH!" and other primal sounds.

Right before Ella dropped back into her chair, she opened her right portal, calling the chameleons back. She became visible within seconds, and as she looked around, she doubted anyone had seen her—at the moment, all attention was on the boy having the conniption.

Richie doubled over, striking the side of a woman's head with his rear end, and flung off his cap. As it hit the ground, the tarsier jumped off, dove through the terrace railing, and disappeared into the treetops.

Richie, realizing he was safe, stood straight and looked around. Seeing everyone's attention on him, he coughed nervously into his fist, attempted a smile, and gave a little bow to his accidental audience. Then he turned around and grabbed his hat before plopping back into his chair.

Before Zak could say a thing, Richie peered across the crowd and pinpointed Ella. Still in her chair, she lifted her palms out to her sides, as if to silently ask him what in the world he was doing. Richie looked away, clearly convinced that she wasn't responsible for this.

"See how much fun that was?" Ella whispered to the Specters. "Remember that for when things get back to normal."

Evie shook her head, pretending to be annoyed. But Ella noticed that part of her grin was showing.

"Man, bro . . ." Zak said. "You were really freaking out."

"There was a tarsier . . . on my head." Richie spoke as if he were explaining something to a thickheaded child.

"Or perhaps you didn't see that?"

"Naw, bro, I saw it. Pretty hard not to."

Richie straightened his cap with two tugs, saying, "That's the second time that's happened, you know."

"Bummer," Zak said. He lifted his gaze to the overhead branches. "Must've fallen out of the trees, you think?"

Richie peered over his shoulder at Ella. "You sure you didn't see her do anything?"

"Naw—she was just sitting there, like she is now."

Richie considered this. "Hmmm. That's the part that makes me nervous."

Zak reached up with an oily hand and adjusted his goggles, which sat on his forehead just below his mismanaged Mohawk. He looked like a nerd who had been through a war. "I think she's got a crush on you, bro."

Richie, who'd just swallowed a chocolate, practically coughed it up. "Excuse me?"

"That girl . . . Ellen . . . I—"

"Ella," Richie corrected.

"Yeah. Her. I think she's diggin' you."

Richie broke out laughing. "You have it *sooo* wrong— trust me."

"C'mon . . . the way she picks on you. I've seen flirting, and that's what it looks like, bro."

Richie plucked a pen from his pocket and pointed its

tip at an electrical component in the box, dismissing the topic. "What's that?"

Zak leaned over. "That's an accelerometer."

"Okay . . ." Richie moved his pen over to a component that looked like a Tic Tac standing on two metal legs. "And this?"

"Ultracapacitor."

He pointed to a circular object with silver tabs. "This?"

"A voltage step-up coil."

"Wow!" Richie said. "You sure know a lot about this thing."

"I should—I built it."

Richie fell back into his chair. "You're serious?"

"Deadly, bro."

"All of it?"

Zak nodded and winked.

"How did you learn so much?"

"Books," Zak said. "Lots and lots of 'em. I do books like other kids do candy—I devour 'em. All the Teks do."

Richie shook his head, astounded. "Are the other Teknikals as smart as you?"

Zak smiled. "You could say we're a high IQ group."

"Are you all the same age?"

"We're different ages, from eighty-seven to eight."

Richie clutched at his chest. "Eight!"

"Morgan. Smartest girl in the group."

Richie leaned across the table so suddenly that his glasses slipped down the bridge of his nose when he came to a stop. "I want to meet her! I want to meet *all* of you!"

Zak shrugged. "Don't see why not." He looked at a dark spot on his hand and seemed to wonder if it was chocolate or dirt before wiping it on a clean spot on his clothes. "Maybe after we get Tank and the others back." He nodded at the electromagical device. "You done with this, bro?"

When Richie nodded, Zak went to work closing it up—a screw here, a clamp there. When the Teknikal was finished, he slid the device aside, accidentally bumping Richie's pen off the table. Before Richie could grab it, the pen rolled along the floor, slipped through the terrace rails, and disappeared into the green, leafy depths.

"Sorry," Zak said.

"No worries, *bro*," Richie said. He liked how natural the word felt coming off his tongue.

"I'm not sure I follow your reasoning," Mr. Darby said as he reached up and adjusted his sunglasses. "Perhaps you can explain again, yes?"

Megan pushed aside a bowl of caramel pecans to make room on the table for her elbows. "I'm just saying . . . the Secret Council shouldn't be the ones to elect new members—the people of the Secret Zoo should do that."

"Are you suggesting that a government chosen by the people will better represent the interests of those people?" Mr. Darby asked.

Megan nodded. "Only in a less fancy way, I guess."

Mr. Darby stroked the tiny head of one tarsier with his fingertip. At last, he said, "And you know this to always be true?"

Megan nodded again, her pigtails wagging.

"Your school . . ." Mr. Darby went on. "You have many students between . . . what? . . . the ages of five and twelve?"

"Something like that."

"What do you suppose your teachers would be like if they were chosen by these young students? Would they be well-suited to teach math, history, and reading? Or would they give extra recesses and show movies during class?"

"Well, yeah, but—"

"We know when to go directly to the people—as we did in the case of your rescue—and we know when to make decisions on behalf of others. Sadly, people sometimes don't know what's best for them."

"And you do? The Secret Council?"

Mr. Darby, still petting the tiny head of the tarsier, softly nodded, saying, "I think so."

"How?" Megan asked.

"Wisdom is something which comes with age."

"Sometimes," Megan said. "Sometimes not."

"Oh?" Mr. Darby said, and Megan realized his tone was growing increasingly curt. "What else might come with age, then?"

"You don't always get smart just by getting old. What if younger people need something different than what you think they need?"

Mr. Darby continued, "People, young and old, need the same things. Food, water, shelter. We need to laugh and love and cry. We need to be a part of something larger than ourselves—part of a family. Some needs are stronger than others. But there is one thing I am certain of. . . ."

As Mr. Darby's voice trailed off, he leaned across the table, coming only a foot or two from Megan's face. From so close, he looked different. Deep lines etched his pale skin, and against the bright white of his beard, his crooked teeth looked yellow and stained. Megan could even smell his breath, and though the odor wasn't strong, it was bad. It was oddly familiar, and Megan realized she'd once experienced something like it. She wondered where, then felt her heart skip a beat when the answer came. In the cellar of Clarksville Elementary—on DeGraff's breath.

". . . there is no greater need than that of revenge," Mr. Darby finished.

Megan didn't like hearing this—not from Mr. Darby.

Up until just now, he seemed too gentle a man.

She stared into his dark sunglasses and tried to see past them, but all she saw were the dim reflections of herself, one in each lens. It suddenly bothered her that none of the scouts had ever seen Mr. Darby's eyes.

Marlo suddenly flew in and landed on Mr. Darby's shoulder. In his beak was a tightly folded slip of paper.

"Thank you, Marlo," Mr. Darby said as he leaned back and took the note. He opened it and read. Then he pushed out his chair and rose from his seat. "Midnight," he announced, and everyone in their group turned to look his way. Solana and the Specters nodded. "Scouts— you should arrive at the Clarksville Zoo no later than eleven-thirty Saturday night. Do you know the employee parking lot?"

The four of them nodded.

"That's where you need to be."

CHAPTER 15

THE OPENING

After supper that night, Mr. and Mrs. Nowicki left for parent-teacher conferences, and dropped Megan off at Ella's on their way. In his room, Noah sat at his desk with a novel in his lap, his thoughts less on the story and more on tomorrow's rescues.

Shortly after eight o'clock, a loud *click!* came from the closet, and he looked up. He waited for more sounds. Slanted light fell into the closet, revealing little more than clothes dangling from hangers.

Click! Click!

The noise again. It seemed too loud to be coming from

the furnace. Maybe the boards in the wall were creaking.

The clicks were followed by a new sound. Something like a groan, but different.

He set down his pen and pushed out his chair, careful not to make a sound. If he walked to the other side of the room, he'd have a better view. On his way across the floor, he scanned his clock: 8:19. How soon before his parents would be home?

He came to a stop when his new angle revealed piles of clothes and shoes. Nothing seemed out of the ordinary. He waited, leaning forward. No further sounds came. What he'd heard must have been the house settling. But still . . . all the weirdness from his closet lately . . . How could he be sure?

Intending to walk back to his desk, he instead found himself moving forward again. He could just peek in, assure himself nothing was wrong.

The floorboards creaked and popped beneath his feet. Just a few steps away from the closet, he stopped and listened. A distant car revved its engine, but nothing else.

He took a deep breath and rolled his shoulders. Then he walked into the closet, where the scene that greeted him stopped him cold. In the wall where the heat vent had been, a velvet curtain the size of a beach towel dangled. A pile of crushed drywall lay beneath it in a cloud of dust. On the shelves and dangling from the racks were monkeys, five of them. Short, daggerlike teeth filled their mouths, claws curled out past their fingertips, and patches of black skin were visible in bald spots along their mangy hair. They stared at Noah with yellow eyes filled with hate.

The velvet curtain swung out as another monkey crawled through the portal, raising the total to six. Two were spider monkeys and the others were howlers, each as black as coal.

Noah took a step back. He might be able to get out and shut the closet door with the same motion, locking the monkeys inside. But he would have to be swift.

One of the monkeys let loose a bloodcurdling squeal, and above its head, its tail curled one way and then another. The other monkeys tensed and prepared to pounce.

Noah grabbed the doorknob and jumped back into his bedroom, swinging the door around with him. But before he could shut the monkeys in, one lunged off a shelf and landed on his chest, the tips of its claws piercing his flesh. Noah let go of the door and grabbed his attacker with both hands, flinging it aside as he stumbled into his room. The other monkeys rushed out of the closet and moved in on Noah, their long tails swinging in the air behind them. They spread out in a half circle, partly surrounding him.

Noah back stepped across the room. "What . . . what do you want?" he heard himself say.

The monkeys couldn't answer, of course, but Noah didn't need them to. What they wanted was him.

As he continued to walk backward, he noticed a wadded-up shirt by his feet. He kicked it toward the monkeys and the shirt opened in the air and fell harmlessly to the carpet—a lame attempt to defend himself.

The monkeys moved in. The howler opened its mouth and did what it was named for, its deep growl like the call of a monster. It jumped up several feet and landed in a new spot.

What could Noah do? The monkeys were blocking his way out, and he couldn't jump from his second-story window. If he tried to fight, the monkeys would tear him to shreds. He didn't keep a phone in his room, and even if he did—

His thoughts stopped. A phone. Though Noah didn't have one, he had something better. A headset—a direct line to the security guards and any Descenders in the Clarksville Zoo. He kept the headset—a tiny earpiece that used bone conduction to carry his voice—in his desk drawer. If he could get to it, he could radio for help.

The monkeys moved to within three feet. They were squealing and grunting and growling, their eyes glowing yellow. The howler jumped out in front of the pack and

Noah kicked at it, just missing its flat face. The startled monkey fell onto its haunches and showed its teeth.

Noah's rear end struck something and he glanced over his shoulder to see that he'd backed into the front of the desk. If he—

His thoughts halted as pain erupted in his chest and shoulders. As he turned his head back around, he came face-to-face with a monkey. He tried to retreat, forgetting he was backed against the desk, which toppled up on two legs and then crashed down, booming against the floor. Papers fluttered around the room like wounded birds, and pens rolled across the carpet. The monkey jumped off his chest as Noah lost his balance and dropped face-down to the ground beside the fallen desk.

Around him lay pens, markers, tape, coins, and index cards. Noah spotted his headset, but as he reached for it, something coiled around his wrist and pulled his arm away. What looked like black rope, Noah realized, was a tail.

As he struggled onto his back, a second monkey whipped out its tail and seized his other wrist. A third and fourth monkey grabbed his ankles. With their tails pulled tight, Noah couldn't move. He felt as if he were tied to four trees, his arms out to his sides, his legs spread wide.

The howler prowled up alongside Noah, its shoulders

rocking, its long tail dragging behind it. It opened its jaw and inched its fangs toward Noah's neck. Noah tried in vain to pull his limbs free as the monkey's warm breath washed over him.

He craned his head up and realized something about one of the spider monkeys holding his ankles. It had the cord of the tall lamp, which was still standing, wrapped around its leg. If Noah could pull the monkey in one direction, the cord might yank down the lamp and distract the other monkeys long enough for him to break free.

He twisted his hips and kicked out with all his strength. The monkey only budged, but it was enough—the cord went taut and the lamp fell like a tree. It crashed down, its bulb shattering in a flash of light and leaving complete darkness. Noah felt his legs and arms released as the monkeys scattered.

He had no chance to locate the headset in the new darkness. His only hope was to get out of the house. He rolled aside, jumped up, and headed across the floor, the monkeys at his feet, their howls and screams echoing off the walls. He slipped through the half-open bedroom door and slammed it shut behind him. Then he sprinted the length of the hallway and practically dove down the steps, his hands on the rails like a gymnast between parallel bars. As he hit the bottom, the bedroom door banged open and the monkeys began to pound their way down the hall. They'd had no problem working the doorknob, and Noah wondered how smart and capable they were now that DeGraff had poured his dark magic into them.

He ran through the kitchen and threw open the back door, but a spider monkey jumped onto the porch, its yellow eyes glowing in the light from the house.

Noah heard a thud and then leaves rustling somewhere in his yard. As a second monkey charged from around the corner of the house, Noah realized what was happening—the animals were jumping out of his bedroom window. He had no idea if these were part of the original six or were new.

He slammed the door shut just as the spider monkey lunged at him, then he heard a series of thuds as it tumbled down the porch steps. Through the door's small window, Noah saw the second monkey leap across its fallen companion and grab at the doorknob, which Noah locked just in time. It squealed, and through the glass Noah saw its black tongue. On the steps, its comrade rose to its feet.

The front door was now Noah's best hope, but as he ran back into the kitchen, so did a group of monkeys from the entrance to the dining room. Squealing and biting at the air, they spread out to surround him. One jumped to a kitchen cart, another to the table, a third to the edge of the countertop. Noah was trapped . . . again.

He backed into the sink and the rattle of the dishes gave him an idea for a weapon. He grabbed a big frying pan still coated in grease from the evening dinner. With the long handle in both hands, he waved it at each of the monkeys, and when this wasn't enough to stop their approach, he batted it against the cabinets, the resulting *toonngggg!* making the monkeys jump back a few feet.

Noah lunged toward the one on the countertop and swung his arm in a wild arc. The pan struck the monkey with a clang, and it fell to the floor and hobbled off toward the back door.

Noah didn't hesitate. He banged the pan against the spider monkey on the table, and with a second swing, he barely missed the monkey on the kitchen cart. Cans of spices flew across the room and shattered against the wall. One of the animals guarding the doorway jumped onto Noah's back and sank its teeth into his shoulder. Noah screamed as pain shot down his arm, and charged backward. He slammed into something—the fridge—and the monkey let go and ran from the room.

He heard the window on the back door smash open, then the rattle of the doorknob as a monkey fumbled with the lock. How many were outside now? Five? Ten? More?

When he raised the pan at the final monkey in his way, it tore from the room, its tail dragging behind it. As Noah ran to the front door, it flew open and monkeys flooded into the house, crawling over the backs of one another.

Noah turned and fled up the stairs. He needed to close the portal! Moonlight had filled his room. As he ran into the closet, he slammed into something—something that had portaled from the Secret Zoo, and something that was too big to be a monkey.

Charlie Red.

CHAPTER 16

THE ATTACK

Noah swung the frying pan but missed Charlie Red, and the steel struck the closet shelves and rang like a weak bell. Charlie plucked the pan from Noah's grasp and lobbed it into the bedroom, where it bounced once and then loudly wobbled to rest. Noah backed out of the closet and Charlie followed, his long limbs swinging from his lanky frame.

From the hallway came the howl and squeal of the monkeys. One by one, they rushed through the door, spotted Charlie, and took posts around the room—on the bed, the fallen desk, the sill of the open window. Their long tails rose above their heads like cobras poised to strike.

Charlie lunged at Noah, who managed to squirm away but tripped on the desk and fell, the side of his head hitting the floor. Around the room, the monkeys began to scream.

Noah stared out at the upended world—one wall acting as the ceiling; another, the floor. In his view lay the things which had spilled out of his desk drawer, and he happened to see his headset. A curvy piece of plastic the size of a marble, it sat beside a wadded ball of paper. As Noah turned onto his back, he swept up the headset and plugged it into his ear as casually as he could.

"Leave me alone!" he screamed, knowing his voice was being carried through the airwaves and into the ears of the Clarksville Zoo security guards. "Charlie—get out of my house!"

Had someone from the Secret Society heard? And if they had, could they possibly respond in time to save his life?

As Charlie stepped up to Noah, three monkeys fell in around him, moonlight glinting on their teeth.

"Out of my house, Red!" Noah repeated.

Charlie dropped onto his knees on Noah's chest, and pain shot through Noah's torso as air was pushed out of his lungs. As Charlie brought down his weight, his head moved into a stream of moonlight. His hair was more red than ever, and his freckles were large and splotchy. The edges of his teeth had begun to decay.

Noah tried to say something more into his bone mic, but without any breath, he couldn't make a sound. He tried to push Charlie off, but it was a wasted effort— Charlie was too strong.

On the floor, the trio of monkeys huddled around to watch. Others looked down from the furniture and the windowsill, their eyes wide and anxious.

"You're coming with me, kid," Charlie said. "My boss wants some more company. Maybe then Darby will come and pay him a visit." He suddenly jumped to his feet, grabbed Noah's ankles, and started to pull him across the floor, the monkeys jumping around with delight.

Noah was too weak to resist. It was all he could do just to breathe.

A monkey on the windowsill suddenly dropped to the floor and began to jump around, swinging its long arms over its shoulders and howling in a panic. With one arm, it pitched something across the room—something that emitted a loud squeak as it hit the carpet. A tarsier— Noah had heard them before. And because hundreds of tarsiers occupied the trees throughout his neighborhood, Noah was certain that many more were coming.

The monkey danced to a new spot and stripped off another tarsier. This one flew directly over Noah, just missing Charlie but startling him enough to get him off balance. Noah drove his feet into Charlie's knees, sending him to the ground.

Tarsiers began to flood through the open window, dozens at a time. They bounded off the sill like frogs and sailed through the room, landing on the bed, the nightstand, the floor. The drapes began to swing as tarsiers clung to their folds.

Charlie screamed and reached for his shoulder, where a tarsier had touched down and was now biting him. As he pulled away the animal, a second one landed on his forearm and bit into his wrist. A third tarsier attacked him—then a fourth, a fifth, a sixth. For a while, Charlie was able to strip them off, but they soon practically covered his body. Charlie ran across the room and into the closet, bumping into the shelves. Noah got to his feet and stumbled after him, but Charlie was gone, and the piece of velvet over the portal was swaying.

Noah turned, and when the room began to spin, he dropped to one knee, surprised by how dazed he was. After a few seconds, he stood again, leaned a shoulder against the frame of the closet door, and tried to steady his gaze on the scene in front of him. Tarsiers were still pouring through the open window. Hundreds were on the floor and furniture. They hopped around like furry frogs, attacking the monkeys with their teeth and powerful hind legs. As the monkeys squealed and bucked and thrashed, Noah was reminded of grasshoppers trying to fend off an army of ants.

Someone stormed into the bedroom and Noah's heart jumped in his chest. The person he felt certain was his mother or father turned out to be Solana. She had her Descender gear down—twelve-inch quills dangling from her arms and the body of her leather jacket. Without breaking her stride, she tore quills from her sleeves, jumped in behind one of the monkeys, and swung her hands down in front of her, tarsiers scattering as she buried the barbs into the creature's neck. She turned and threw the same quills into the chest of another monkey, which staggered and fell to the floor. Solana turned left . . . right. She spotted a third monkey off to one side of the room, and she sprang on and off the bed, her long hair sweeping the ceiling before she came down and punched her barbed knuckles into its chest.

In the space of a few seconds, Solana did what she'd been bred to do—she'd made prey of her adversaries. Words that Noah had once read from a dictionary rose in his head. To *descend* meant "to pounce upon—to attack with violence and suddenness." This was what the Descenders did best.

The remaining monkeys jumped over Noah and disappeared through the portal in the closet. Solana chased after them and ripped away the curtain. Immediately, the pieces of drywall rose into the air, the hole in the wall closed, and the ordinary heat vent appeared.

She pulled Noah away from the closet into the open air of the room, tarsiers scattering to avoid them. When Noah lost his balance and fell, she sat on her heels and laid his head on the makeshift pillow of her knees. Then she retracted the quills on her hands and began to fan his face with her fingers.

"You okay?"

Noah looked up and realized the world was still wavering. He saw Solana—her long hair, her dark eyes. Tarsiers had crawled across her limp quills to stare down on Noah; at least a dozen pairs of eyes were on him. She stroked his cheek with the back of her hand and then ran her fingers through his hair.

"Noah—answer me!"

He managed a weak nod.

Tarsiers continued to crowd Noah from around the room. He felt the light patter of their feet as a few climbed onto his legs and chest. Then he felt something warm streaming out of his nose. Blood.

Solana shook her head and looked away. When her gaze returned, Noah saw a tear had formed in the corner of her eye.

And that was when Noah heard the front doorbell ring.

CHAPTER 17

A NEIGHBORLY VISIT

"**G**et up!" Solana said, keeping her shout to a whisper.

The ring of the doorbell echoed through the house a second time.

Solana stood and pulled Noah to his feet. "Someone's here!" she said. "It could be the police!"

Noah stared at his room, where hundreds of tarsiers sat perched on the bed, the dressers, the curtain rod, the top of the closet door. With their big eyes on Noah and Solana, they seemed to comprehend the new danger. On the floor lay three dead monkeys, and beneath them, blood was on the carpet.

Ding-doonngg . . . A third time now, the sound echoing up the stairs.

Solana retracted all of her Descender gear and dragged Noah into the hallway and then the bathroom. Beside the bathtub, Solana balanced him on his unsteady feet, raised her hand, and shot up a single quill from her knuckles. She swiped the point of the quill from Noah's neck to his ankle, slicing his clothes on the way. Then she pulled and twisted Noah out of his shirt and pants, leaving him standing in his boxer shorts, his heels against the bathtub. Despite his pain and dizziness, Noah's cheeks flushed as he realized he was nearly naked.

Behind Noah, the roar of the shower started. Then he swung back into the spray, Solana gripping his shoulders. Water blinded him and filled his mouth, along with the copper taste of his blood. He lost his breath to the cold, and then was pulled out of the shower again, where he stood blinking, his senses awake.

Solana stripped a towel off the rack and tied it around his waist. Then she checked his nose and apparently saw it was no longer bleeding. "Go."

Noah almost asked "Where?" and then he heard the doorbell ring again. He walked out of the bathroom and headed into the hall, leaving wet footprints in the carpet.

"Get whoever that is out of here," Solana said.

Noah nodded. He listened for the "*eeps!*" of the tarsiers

and realized he couldn't hear a thing. After making his way through the house, he opened the front door, and out on the porch stood Mr. Connolly, the neighbor from across the street who came knocking so often these days.

"Noah?" Mr. Connolly said. "Everything okay over here?"

Noah feigned a look of confusion.

"The noise," Mr. Connolly said. "I was coming over to say hi to your parents and I heard a terrible racket coming from your house—your bedroom, it sounded like."

"Huh? Oh, the music. I was in the shower with the stereo on. Sorry—I think my window's open a crack."

Mr. Connolly raised an eyebrow and leaned a bit sideways to peer past Noah. "Your parents home?"

Noah shook his head.

"Mind if I come in?"

Noah tried to protest, but Mr. Connolly wormed his way around him and headed into the living room.

"Mr. Connolly, I don't think—"

"Megan here?"

"She's at Ella's."

Mr. Connolly grunted. He looked around the room and then at Noah. With one side of his mouth frowning, he sized him up.

"You sure everything's okay?"

Noah nodded; a bit anxiously, he realized.

Mr. Connolly waited a few seconds, then said, "How's everything at school?"

"Ummm . . ." It seemed totally weird for Mr. Connolly to ask such a casual question. Noah, after all, was standing almost naked in his living room, water dripping from his hair. "Okay, I guess."

"No problems? Your teachers treating you okay?"

"Uh-huh."

"Friends . . . they're good?"

Noah nodded.

"Mr. Connolly, I . . . I really need to dry off."

"Mind if I have a look around?"

Noah tried to answer, but his neighbor brushed past his shoulder and headed toward the stairs.

"Mr. Connolly!"

The old man pressed a straight, knuckly finger against the tip of his lips—a gesture for Noah to be quiet.

As his neighbor rushed up the steps, Noah chased after him. "Mr. Connolly—everything's okay! I'm not—"

But before Noah could do anything more, Mr. Connolly was standing at his open bedroom door.

CHAPTER 18

ALL TIDIED UP

"Mr. Connolly! I can—"

Noah's words stopped short when he saw that his room was perfectly clean. The tarsiers, the monkeys, the stains on the carpet—all of it was gone. Every piece of Noah's furniture stood upright, and even the lamp with the once-broken bulb was glowing again.

Mr. Connolly looked around, then poked his head in the closet. Seeing nothing out of the ordinary, he turned to Noah. "I'm sorry. I thought . . . I thought for certain someone was in here and you were being forced to stay quiet. The noise coming from your bedroom—I've never heard anything like it."

Noah walked over to his stereo, which had been turned on and was now playing low, and switched it off. "I had it too loud, so I could hear it in the shower. I'm sorry I freaked you out."

Mr. Connolly's face flushed. "You see things on the news . . . kidnappings and stuff. Heck—we all thought it happened to your sister when she got trapped in that Jackson House. I guess . . . I guess I'm still jumpy."

"I'm okay," Noah said. "If someone was here, I'd tell you right now, believe me."

The old man turned and left the room. Noah followed him through the house and to the front door, where he finally left after more apologies and explanations. Noah latched the door behind him and took a deep, needed breath. Then he ran upstairs and burst back into his room, which was still empty, still perfectly clean.

"Solana?" he said.

Solana stepped through the doorway behind him, and Noah realized she must have been hiding in another bedroom. An instant after she appeared, so did a second person, who Noah recognized as a Constructor, a person trained to use magic to repair damage caused to the outside world. In one of his hands was a small duffle bag; in the other, a piece of velvet the size of a towel.

"We all set here?" the Constructor asked.

"I think we're good," Solana answered.

The Constructor stuffed the velvet into his bag, saying,

"See you at base." He nodded at Noah, turned, and hurried downstairs. Seconds later, the back door slammed.

"When you were talking to your neighbor, he slipped in through a window. I radioed for him on my way over. He took care of the kitchen, too."

Noah nodded. Realizing he still had little more than a towel wrapped around him, he went into the closet, threw on some sweatpants and a T-shirt, then stepped back out into the room. Solana grabbed his chin and moved his head to one side, then the other.

"No marks," she said. "That's good." She squinted into his eyes and added, "You all right?"

Noah nodded again.

She lowered her hand. "Once I portal, I'll radio Council and have them post Specters near Ella's and Richie's. And we'll beef up the patrol—keep you safe."

Noah nodded a third time.

"Keep your headsets close—you and Megan both. I doubt DeGraff will move again tonight, but if he does, you need to be ready." Solana went to the open window and stared across the street. "Your neighbor—think he'll be watching you now?"

Noah shook his head. "He trusts me. I've known Mr. Connolly all my life. He's a good man."

"Then I'm glad you stalled him long enough for your room to be reconstructed."

This confused Noah, and all he managed in response was a breathy "Huh?"

Before Solana could respond, a noise came from downstairs—the rattle of the front doorknob as a key fitted into its slot. From the open window, Noah heard his mother's voice.

"Kill the lights," Solana said. As she sat on the windowsill, Noah realized she had the portal curtain balled up in one hand. "Remember—keep your headset close, just in case. I can be here in seconds."

"Wait!" Noah heard himself say.

Solana turned to him. "Yeah?"

Noah wanted to say so much, but hearing his parents' footsteps downstairs, he knew there wasn't time. He settled on what he thought was most important. "I . . . I'm scared."

Just when Noah felt certain a response wouldn't come, she said, "You should be."

Noah took a step back, surprised at the truth, which was the last thing he'd expected to hear.

"Your headset—keep it close," she reminded him again. Then, in one swift movement, she swung her legs out the window and dropped out of sight.

Noah lay there, unable to sleep. He kept gazing at the closet. What if another portal opened? What if Charlie came back? Solana had instructed Noah to keep his headset close, but he'd done more than that—he was wearing it. To reach the Descenders, all he needed to do was push a button.

Noah looked toward the window and imagined Solana there. His thoughts drifted to Tarsier Terrace and the conversation they'd had. She'd been so distracted and worried. Her friends' lives were in the hands of six girls she didn't trust. Were the Specters really capable of leaving the Descenders behind?

The Descenders want revenge, Solana had said. *But the Specters . . . they want it even more.*

The idea of Sam and Hannah and Tameron being abandoned made Noah sick. How many times had the Descenders come to his aid? If only Noah could help them now. But of course, Blizzard and Little Bighorn needed Noah just as much as the Descenders, and if the scouts—

He focused on a spot in the room. The scouts—Richie, Ella, Megan, and him. Four friends for two missions.

He sat up and gazed at the floor. An idea stuck him and he jumped to his feet and paced the room, thoughts swirling in his head.

Four friends for two missions.

He walked to the window and looked out. When he remembered Solana and the way she'd come to his rescue tonight, he realized that he owed her the same.

CHAPTER 19

LEAVING HOME

Noah spent Saturday with fear and adrenaline coursing through him. Tonight, he and his friends would be participating in a secret rescue mission while other kids were fast asleep in their beds. It hardly seemed possible.

At six o'clock that evening, he made his way into the kitchen for dinner. Eggs, bacon, hash browns, toast—breakfast food, which meant tomorrow was grocery day. Megan was in her normal seat at the table, her hair up in pigtails.

Noah chomped down on a piece of bacon made bland by his worry. When his parents were out of earshot at the cupboards, he leaned toward his sister and softly said, "You ready?"

Megan shrugged, then nodded, then shrugged again. She bit into an egg and chewed, perhaps to avoid having to talk. Just hours ago, she'd agreed to go along with Noah's new plan.

"Did you call Ella?" Noah asked.

Megan nodded.

"And?"

"She's good with it."

Noah's gaze wandered to the fridge and the different pieces of paper stuck on it: a telephone bill, his report card, a coupon for the new go-kart track in town.

The go-kart track. A normal place normal kids might go. But not Noah and Megan—not tonight.

The thought made a mess of his feelings. He concentrated on the crunch his toast made in his ears and studied a smudge on the table. Eventually though, his gaze lifted and happened upon the row of photographs across the wall. Megan as an infant, his mother in a summer dress. Pictures from weddings, holidays, and vacations—moments of lives well lived, and of people well loved.

Noah turned to the clock: 6:16. He couldn't help but wonder how much danger he and Megan were in, and a new thought struck him. What if he and his sister walked away from all this and revealed the Secret Zoo to their parents? What if they just spilled the truth about what they'd been doing at the Clarksville City Zoo, and about what happened in their tree fort at night?

"No," Megan said. She'd been watching Noah and reading his thoughts in a strange way that only siblings can. "We can do this—we're ready."

She glanced over at their parents, who were currently raiding one cabinet, noisily moving things around as they searched for something—probably the Tabasco sauce, which their father loved on his eggs.

"We could—"

"No," Megan interrupted. "We can't."

After dinner, Noah and Megan headed upstairs to pack for their sleepovers. On his way out the bedroom door, Noah found himself checking the closet again. Nothing—the portal was still gone.

At seven o'clock, they were ready. Before heading to the door, they stopped at the kitchen, where their parents were still at the table, drinking tea.

"When will you be back?" their mother asked.

"Early," Megan said. "Before lunch."

Noah hated the way it felt like a lie, and he hated the way it made his heart sting.

"Be safe," their mother said.

Noah ran forward, wrapped his arms around his mother, and hugged her tight.

"Whoa!" his mother said as she stabilized herself. She hugged him back. "I'm not sure what that's for . . . but I'll take it."

Megan and Noah took turns hugging their father and then headed for the door, adjusting the packs on their backs. As they went, Noah deliberately kept his gaze away from the family pictures on the wall.

They began walking the short distance to Ella and Richie's. As they rounded a turn, Noah chanced a look back at his house. It seemed different in ways he didn't understand. His house, which normally looked so full of life, seemed vacant, not just of people, but everything. No furniture, no walls—as hollow as a building on a Hollywood set.

"Don't," Megan cautioned. "Stay focused."

His sister did something totally unexpected then. She reached out and grabbed his hand, threading his fingers through hers.

Noah chanced another look back. His house suddenly looked less fake and more like a place from a dream that he was already forgetting.

CHAPTER 20

THE WAY TO WATERFORD

Solana peered through the darkness to read the words on the short semitrailer: "Caution! Live Animals!" It was the vehicle the Clarksville Zoo used to transport animals. In the driver's seat was a hefty man with broad shoulders and a round, weighty head—Mike, a Secret Cityzen who lived on the Outside. He greeted Solana with a nod.

Solana jumped to the bumper and stepped through the trailer's open back door. Two rows of fluorescent lights dimly lit the large space. The trailer had three benches, one on each side. The Specters were sitting, two girls to a bench. One bench that ran along the cab of the truck was empty.

"Where are the scouts?" Solana asked.

"Right here," Megan said, and her voice came from the vacant seats. The scouts were already ghosted.

"Practice," Richie chimed in. "We want to be ready."

Solana took an open seat beside Jordynn, who promptly slid down the bench a couple of feet. Solana scanned the group of girls, but none of them would meet her gaze.

She realized it was going to be a long drive.

After the meeting in the Room of Reflections, Mr. Darby had asked Solana to go along on the rescue in case the Specters got into trouble, but none of the Specters had liked the idea. In the end, Solana had agreed to stay in the vehicle unless needed.

Mike appeared at the back of the truck, his bulbous belly quaking with every movement. "We set, ladies?"

Sara was the only one to respond, and she did so with a quick nod.

Mike grabbed the strap dangling from the top-loading door. "Hope you girls are ready for this." He pulled down his arm and the door groaned and slammed shut.

In the confined space, the few sounds were louder: the buzz of a dying fluorescent bulb, the *tick, tick* of Jordynn picking at her nails, the groan of the bench as Lee-Lee leaned back and kicked out her feet. Someone coughed into her fist. Kaleena. Someone else grunted. Seconds later, the engine turned over, and its growl made the walls tremble. The truck jerked forward as it pulled out of the parking lot. Then the girls rocked in their seats as Mike made a series of turns before finally driving onto the steady stretch of Walkers Boulevard.

Solana swept her long black hair off her shoulders. To avoid eye contact with the other girls, she stared down at her leather gloves. She'd never been alone with the Specters for more than a few minutes. Had any of the Descenders?

She forced her eyes to rise. On the bench in front of her sat Sara and Lee-Lee, busy stuffing a backpack with a stack of paper—pages which read, "Free them or we will!" in bold gold font. When Lee-Lee noticed Solana watching her, she handed a few flyers over to her. Solana folded the papers into a square and crammed them into her jacket pocket. Lee-Lee then dished out a few to the other girls.

"I'm sorry," Solana suddenly heard herself say. "For what happened, I mean. I wish. . . ." Her voice trailed off as she realized she didn't know what to say. "I wish someone could have stopped it."

The truck made a wide turn and everyone jostled in their seats.

"We didn't know," Solana said. "We didn't. And then it just happened and it was too late. Your families . . . friends . . . I'm just . . . so sorry."

The Specters said nothing. Lee-Lee and Kaleena looked away.

Solana opened her mouth and then closed it. There was no point in this. Not now. Not with so much else to worry about. Now, she had to focus, to channel her own hurt and aggression and do something meaningful with it. This was something the Descenders did best. The Specters, after all, weren't the only ones who had suffered.

The truck drove on and on. Then it finally pulled off the expressway and soon slowed to a stop. With a flick of her wrist, Sara killed the fluorescent lights. Lee-Lee and Kaleena laced their arms through the straps of their backpacks. Footsteps moved alongside the trailer, then the big door squealed open and dim moonlight spilled into the surrounding space. The silhouette of a man appeared.

"Welcome to the Waterford Zoo," Mike said. "You're clear to go." He turned and quickly walked back to the cab.

As the Specters rose from their seats, Richie shouted, "Wait!" from his place of invisibility toward the front of the truck.

"What is it?" Sara asked.

After a long pause, Richie said, "There's something . . . something we have to tell you."

The Specters stayed quiet. Then they turned and listened.

CHAPTER 21

FINAL PREP

"Are we ready?" Mr. Darby asked.

Evie looked up and caught her own image reflected twice in the dark lenses of the old man's sunglasses. "We're ready."

Evie and Elakshi were standing in front of Mr. Darby, who was seated at a table in Lots of Latte, a coffee shop a few buildings down from the gateway into the Secret Creepy Critters. The nearby streets had been reopened since Mr. Darby ordered them closed days ago, and Evie saw people watching, giraffes lifting their heads above signs, and monkeys peering from multistory windows.

Everyone knew what was about to take place, but they were careful not to make a spectacle, just in case someone—DeGraff or one of his minions—was watching.

Mr. Darby reached under a nearby table and brought out two backpacks. One was immediately recognizable—Tameron's pack, the one with the magical tail—but the other wasn't. Mr. Darby handed the latter over to Evie, saying, "The Descenders' gear—everything I could fit."

Evie nodded and slipped her arms through the straps. As she did, Elakshi scooped up Tameron's larger pack.

Mr. Darby said, "Ten minutes to the Core, five minutes to rescue the Cityzens, ten more to get out."

Evie nodded. They'd reviewed and rehearsed the plan dozens of times.

"And if you don't return within a half hour," Mr. Darby continued, "we'll send in Marlo to check on you. If he brings back bad news, we'll send backup—as many Descenders as we can afford to pull off guard. Our animals, too. We won't abandon you in that place." He looked at a clock on the wall and added, "Operation Rescue is scheduled to begin in five minutes. Any last thoughts or considerations?"

"What if I get a shot at bringing down DeGraff," Evie said. "Should I take it?"

Mr. Darby quickly shook his head. "Just get in and out. This is a rescue mission—nothing else."

Evie gave a quick nod and unzipped her left portal pocket, prompting Elakshi to do the same. Chameleons scuttled out from the magical depths onto their torsos and limbs, and the two of them faded into the surroundings.

"Stay close," Evie said to Elakshi. "Follow my marks, but leave none."

As Evie pushed through the exit, Elakshi was close behind her. After a few seconds, she glanced back at Mr. Darby and happened to see that the door hadn't closed behind Elaskshi—it was still partly open, as if someone was in its way.

But of course, no one was, and a second later the door eased shut.

CHAPTER 22

SOLANA'S SHOCK

In the dimly lit truck parked alongside the Waterford Zoo, Solana looked back and forth between Sara and the scouts. A part of her wanted to believe that what she was seeing wasn't real—that the scouts couldn't have done something so reckless. Sara stood there, her face full of shock. The other Specters looked frozen in place.

Sara took a slow, cautious step toward the scouts. She stopped. After a long silence, she came out with the exact question that Solana wanted to ask, her voice quiet so Mike couldn't hear.

"What . . . what have you done?"

◈ CHAPTER 23 ◈

THE PATH TO THE CREEPY CORE

Evie and Elakshi slipped through the portal into the Secret Creepy Critters, turning their shoulders to disturb the curtains as little as possible. A slant of light came through with them, but anyone seeing it would surely think it was the wind blowing the curtains apart.

Inside, the world was pitch-black, just as it had been in Marlo's video. Evie wrinkled her nose at the musty, filthy smell all around. Something crunched beneath her foot—an insect, no doubt, and a rather large one. When she lifted her leg, guts stuck to the sole of her shoe. She heard the click and clatter of other bugs scrambling on the floor, the ceiling, the walls.

She moved through the darkness a single step at a time, her hands held forward, her fingers probing the air. She began to hear the same low growls they'd heard in the video. On either side of them were sasquatches, and she listened for distinct rumbles and guessed their number. Three? Six? Ten? All she knew for certain was that they were along the walls on both sides.

A beetle the size of her thumb fell on her head and then crawled onto her face. She sucked back her breath to stifle a scream and swatted the thing aside. Then she tried to overcome her fear by concentrating again on her walk.

Before long, a dimly lit intersection came into view, and she led Elakshi right into a new corridor that was partly illuminated by torches. Spiders, millipedes, and cockroaches roamed the walls. Moths, locusts, and other insects were flying. They bumped off Evie's cheeks and chin, and one slipped past her lips, its wings fluttering against her tongue before she could spit it out.

A single sasquatch came into view. It sat with its back against the wall, its elbows propped on its raised knees. Bugs squirmed along its body and tunneled through its mangy hair. As Evie walked by it, a particularly large insect burst beneath her foot, making the loudest pop yet, and the sasquatch raised its head. She kept perfectly still as the beast sniffed the air and slowly turned its head in one direction, then the other. It curled up one end of its lip, exposing a tusklike fang, and gave a low growl that rumbled beneath the noise of the insects. Just as Evie became certain it was about to attack, a giant millipede emerged from the fur on its forehead and crawled over one of its eyes. The sasquatch snorted and snatched the millipede, which it stuffed into its mouth and chewed to pieces before spitting out the remains. Then it wiped its chin with the back of its hand and looked down, presumably having forgotten about the noise Evie had made.

Evie started off again and soon made a new turn. This hall seemed a continuation of the previous, with broken aquariums set in bug-covered walls. But there were hardly any bugs in the next corridor, and the walls had more aquariums, about half of which were still intact, fish swimming around bubbling streams of air from the filters. The other aquariums were broken and vacant, their black innards looking like the open mouths of monsters. Evie knew where they were now—the Secret Zoo's version of Fish Foyer. On one side of the floor lay a sasquatch, sleeping, and Evie held her breath when she caught a whiff of its sewerlike stench.

The next corridor soon appeared. She moved through it quickly, then through the next and the next, mindful to mark her position to Elakshi: a kick of her foot through the insects; a sweep of her hand through the smoke of a torch.

When she neared the doorway to the Secret Legless Lane, Elakshi grunted in pain. Evie turned and marked her friend by what she saw along the floor. A snake was whipping around, involuntarily, and it was obvious that it had bitten Elakshi, who was trying to shake it off. Elakshi cried out for Evie, her scream held to a whisper.

Evie ran back, hoisted her foot, and brought it down, hard. The snake's mouth sprang open, and in the flickering light of a flame, Evie saw its blood-tinted fangs, which were still dripping poison. It crawled off as fast as it could, a kink in its long, sinuous body. By its striped pattern, Evie knew it was a blue krait, one of the Secret Zoo's deadliest snakes.

Evie dropped to one knee and held Elakshi, who'd fallen.

"What was that?" Elakshi said, and Evie heard something in her voice that she rarely did. Fear.

"A krait," Evie said. "Elakshi—you have to go back. You need a doctor."

"No!" Elakshi said. "I can—"

"You *can't*," Evie shot back. "You know that, and there's no time to argue. Give me the gear."

Evie could tell Elakshi's reluctance by how long it took her to make any noise. But before long, she heard the backpack slide across the ground toward her, and then the scuttle of feet as a few chameleons crawled off it and back onto Elakshi. It took only seconds for the pack to appear, and then the girls stood.

"How are you going to carry it?" Elakshi asked.

Evie realized she didn't have an answer. "Don't worry about it. Just go."

Elakshi didn't move, not at first. But Evie soon saw her marks in the long corridor as she limped away.

Silence. Evie was by herself now. She looked down at Tameron's gear and realized there was no way she could carry it—not with the other backpack already strapped over her shoulders. Maybe she could leave it here and pick it up on the way out. But what if they were forced in a different direction? What if they—

Her thoughts stopped and her gaze locked on the backpack, which was no longer lying on the floor, but rising into the air, as if by magic, one of its straps pulled tight.

CHAPTER 24

INTO THE WATERFORD ZOO

Megan stood beside Richie, neither one moving. Solana and the Specters continued to stare at them in shock.

"What's going on?" Sara said.

The scouts had come out of their camouflage to reveal that only two of them were in the truck. Richie was with Megan, but not Noah and Ella.

"They went with Evie," Megan said. "Into Creepy Critters. To help."

"*What?*" Sara said. "Does she . . . does she know?"

Megan shook her head.

Sara took a step forward. "You've got to be *kidding* me!" She looked around the trailer as she searched her thoughts. "They *snuck* in? With Evie?"

"*Behind* Evie," Richie said. "Technically speaking."

Sara kicked one of the benches, almost toppling it. Then she reached toward Solana. "Give me your headset."

Solana took a step back.

"Your *headset*," Sara repeated. "I'm calling this in."

"It's too late," Megan said. "They're already in Creepy Critters."

Sara shifted her eyes and ran her fingers through her wild hair. She kicked the bench a second time.

"They can help," Megan said. "Noah . . . he wanted to help."

"And he was *going* to help!" Sara said. "*Us!*"

Solana took a step in front of the scouts, saying, "Sara—it's too late to call this in. We're here. Let's concentrate on what needs to be done."

Sara opened her mouth, perhaps to protest, and then closed it. After a few seconds, she said to Megan, "You two better keep up." And then she turned and jumped to the ground. The other Specters followed, one after another.

Solana glanced at the scouts, nodded, and then stepped to the side of the truck.

"C'mon, Richie," Megan said. "Let's go."

They jumped through the open loading door, and then landed on the ground, running. Moonlight glinted on the chain-link fence that wound around the perimeter of the Waterford Zoo. At least fifteen feet high, it had rows of barbed wire across its top, their pointy spikes doing less to keep animals in and more to keep people out. For the Specters, this was barely an obstacle, and as they charged up to it, Kaleena reached into her backpack and pulled out a canvas tarp. She heaved it up and onto the barbed wire, and then the fence rattled and clanked as the Specters scaled it one after another, dropping down into the zoo. Megan followed with ease, and even Richie managed without much trouble.

As they neared the first overhead light, Sara said, "Ghost it!"

The Specters reached down and unzipped the left pockets on their cargo pants, and chameleons scrambled out and scattered across their bodies. Megan and Richie followed suit.

Sara said, "We've got a change of plans now that some of us decided not to show. I'll take Megan to get Blizzard. Lee-Lee, you take Richie to Little Big. Everyone else handle the security cams. And remember—we've probably got two guards on foot."

They broke in different directions. Sara and Megan cut through gardens, their warm breath wafting into the cold air like puffs of smoke, and ran beside fountains with statues of animals. They charged past zoo exhibits: Chimpville, Zebra Zone, and Platypus Plunge. In no time they reached the hospital, an old two-story building with canvas awnings and a sprawling courtyard. Somewhere inside it, Blizzard was being kept.

"This is it," Sara said to the empty space beside her.

"Let's go," the space—Megan—responded.

Without slowing their stride, the two girls ran up to the main entrance of the building and prepared to break and enter.

CHAPTER 25

LEGLESS LANE

"Elakshi?" Evie asked.

"It's me," Noah said. "And Ella, too."

"*What?* How did—"

"We followed you," Ella said, and for Noah, it felt good to hear her voice, and he was glad that he hadn't had to do this on his own. The morning after making his decision to help Solana, he'd called Ella and asked for her help. She'd been reluctant, at first, but then Noah convinced her that Tank and the Descenders might be in real danger.

Now Noah watched Tameron's gear settle into position

on Ella's invisible body as she fed her arms through the wide straps. Chameleons crawled onto the pack and quickly blended the pack into the surroundings.

"You can't—"

"Look," Ella said. "We snuck in because we thought you might need help. And good thing we did because Elakshi tapped out. Let's do our job and get out of this nightmare."

Silence. After almost a minute, Noah said, "Evie?"

More silence. Then, at last, Evie said, "Okay, whatever. But Darby finds out this was your idea when we get back!"

"Fair enough."

"Let's go," Evie said. "Follow my marks and stay close, just like we practiced in the zoo."

Evie took a few steps and turned onto Legless Lane. As Noah followed her, he stopped in his tracks. There were far more snakes than Marlo's video had shown—so much more that the floor had no open spots. Their dry scales looked slimy in the wavering light of the flames, and as they hissed and rattled, their tongues flicked in and out.

A handful of tiny objects flew through the air, tumbled down on the bodies of the snakes, and began to stream light all around. Flashmites—Evie must have thrown them. The mites crawled in various directions, parting the snakes. Evie squatted and carefully placed another handful of Zak's invention into one of the clearings, and they began to crawl forward, opening a wide path.

Evie said, "Hold hands. And stay close."

Ella, who was second in line, groped for Noah's arm, his wrist, his fingers. Her cold hand closed around his and then she pulled him along as she stepped into the opening. The head of a cobra sprang up with its hood flattened and its forked tongue whipping around. It began to sway back and forth, and then struck at one of the tiny flashmites, missing completely.

The mechanical bugs continued to divide the snakes and provide a route. As soon as Noah stepped out of Legless Lane, the mites began to fade, and Noah realized their power was already dying. The Crossers then headed into what looked like a huge mountain cavity. The Secret Creepy Core. Noah stopped and looked around at the waterfalls, streams, and stalactites. Aquariums were set in the rocky walls, broken panes of glass giving way to empty innards. Giant insects skittered and squirmed across the floor.

In the middle of the room, glass walls enclosed the Secret Croc Crater. Deep inside of it, Tank and the Descenders were being held prisoner.

Noah felt a tug on his arm and realized Evie was on the move again.

❦ CHAPTER 26 ❧

✦ Horns Aplenty ✦

The rhino exhibit, Horns Aplenty, was in a two-story stone building wrapped in ivy. Lee-Lee and Richie ran past the main doors and squirmed through a row of overgrown hedges to an entrance at the back. The wide door was kept locked, but Lee-Lee had a key—a magical key from the Secret Zoo that could change its shape to fit the dimensions of any lock. As Lee-Lee stood with her back to the door to keep an eye out, she handed the key over her shoulder to Richie, who put it to work. The heavy door swung open, and the two of them slipped inside. Richie held the key out to Lee-Lee, who snatched it back and casually clipped it to a belt loop in her pants.

They'd entered directly into the living quarters of the animals. Moonlight fell through large skylights, revealing the room in shadowy shapes. Three of the surrounding concrete walls were made to look like rocky mountainsides with steep ledges, narrow cliffs, and shallow caves. Fake boulders were scattered across a dirt floor, and a weak waterfall emptied into a shallow wading pool, its ceaseless splash the only sound. About fifty feet away, steel bars stretched from the floor to the ceiling and spanned the length of the building. Beyond them was the viewing area. Across the ground lay a shadowy mound. A rhino.

Richie stared over his shoulder and checked the door they'd entered through. Was it big enough to fit their animal friend? It had better be.

"Is that him?" Lee-Lee whispered.

Richie shrugged, then remembered Lee-Lee couldn't see him. "It's too dark—I can't tell."

"Follow me," said Lee-Lee.

As Lee-Lee headed deeper into the exhibit, Richie followed her marks. She approached the sleeping rhino, which had its legs curled up beneath its hulking mass. Richie crouched low and stared at the rhino's face. He tipped his head from side to side, hunting in the darkness for the animal's features. He saw its ears, its nostrils, the smooth curve of its horn.

The rhino's eyes sprang open, and Richie's heart dropped as its gaze locked on him. Richie was almost certain it couldn't see him—but could it smell him?

Richie waited . . . and waited. He became aware of the chameleons on his body, the patter and pull of their tiny claws.

The rhino twitched all over and then heaved itself upright. Richie realized it was too small to be Little Bighorn.

Richie took a step back, and then another. He winced as a twig snapped beneath his foot. The rhino's dark eyes moved in his direction, and so did its horn. Richie stood perfectly still, feeling his heart drum. The rhino advanced, searching the area with a slow turn of its head.

Just off to Richie's right, someone whistled. Lee-Lee. The rhino quickly veered her way, its head moving into a beam of moonlight, a shadow falling from its horn. When Lee-Lee whistled a second time, it was softer than before, and Richie realized she was moving across the exhibit, luring the rhino away. And then Richie saw something. One end of the wading pool was directly behind the Specter, and if she was paying too much attention to the rhino, she might not know it was there.

Before Richie could do anything, the water splashed and Lee-Lee became a ghostly form waist deep in the pool. Richie wondered why her camouflage was failing and then saw ripples in the water—chameleons swimming.

The rhino charged into the pool, splashing water over its body. Richie saw Lee-Lee's head rock back and then she was pulled directly under the animal, which charged over her without slowing down and then stomped up onto the other shore, where it swung around and stared back into the pool.

As the water slowly stilled, Richie couldn't see the chameleons or Lee-Lee. He searched the shore for watery footprints and found none. Had the Specter gotten out? Or had she—

He noticed movement in the near-still water. Bubbles—a stream of them. He tiptoed forward and saw Lee-Lee's body half floating in the water, her legs dragging on the bottom of the pool, her fingers dangling from her outstretched hands. She was unconscious. On the other side of the pool, the rhino saw her, too.

Richie had a minute—maybe seconds—to save her life. But if he went into the water to pull her out, the rhino would spot him, too. And then they might both die.

✿ CHAPTER 27 ✿

THE ZOO HOSPITAL

"**C**rap!" Sara said.

"What's wrong?" Megan asked.

The two were standing at the front entrance of the zoo hospital. Sara had just punched a series of numbers into a keypad which secured the door.

Sara bounced a fingertip across the buttons again. "The code . . . it's not working."

"Maybe you entered it wrong—"

"No. I tried twice. It must have been changed."

Megan stared down at the locked door. "Stand back."

"Huh?"

She bumped Sara aside with her hip and produced a key, which slid easily into the lock. When she turned her wrist, the door popped open.

"You guys aren't the only ones with a key to this town," Megan said. She'd been carrying the magic key—the key that Tank had secretly delivered to Noah on the night the scouts had discovered the Secret Zoo—since Noah had given it to her on Halloween night.

Sara brushed past Megan to get through the door, and Megan dropped the key back into one of her normal pockets and followed.

The inside air smelled of animals, and cinder-block walls were painted a lifeless hospital gray. A hallway continued straight for about thirty feet before branching in two directions.

"C'mon," Sara said.

In the dim light, Megan could faintly see the Specter— or her basic form, anyway. She looked like a ghost, and Megan knew that Sara had sent back a few chameleons to deliberately mark herself.

The girls continued up the hallway and turned down the right branch, where the cinder blocks were replaced by steel bars that divided a big space into individual rooms. Cages—at least ten on each side. Some were small and others as large as prison cells. On their straw-covered floors, different animals slept. A koala, an aardvark, a chimp.

"I don't see—"

But then Megan did see. In the last cage on the left was Blizzard, sleeping on his side. As the girls rushed down the hall, a few startled animals swung their heads in their direction.

Blizzard looked weak, lying on the floor. And a good deal thinner. Squares of thick gauze were heavily taped to two bare spots on his side. Flimsy bits of straw were threaded through his white fur.

"Bliz!" Megan said.

The bear's eyes eased open and he stared, confused, at the space in front of him.

"Over here!"

Blizzard raised his long neck and looked over toward the sound.

Megan pushed the cage door. Locked. She grabbed her magic key and fitted it into the slot. The heavy door swung inward, groaning on dry hinges.

Sara grabbed her shoulder. "Stop!" she said in a whisper filled with the urgency of a scream.

"What? What are—"

"Shh!"

The girls froze in place and listened. Footsteps. Someone appeared at the branch in the hall, turned, and headed their way. A guard. He had a thin mustache, thin lips, and beady eyes. When he saw the open cage, he halted so suddenly that his narrow frame almost toppled over. For what seemed a long time, he stood perfectly still. Then he lifted a walkie-talkie to his mouth and pressed the button to transmit his voice.

CHAPTER 28

THE GHOST

Jordynn and Kaleena gathered by the three small administrative buildings near the main gates of the zoo. Inside the middle building, they knew, a guard sat in front of a wall of monitors, each one showing a different area of the property in flickering black and white. The Specters' objective: remove the guard from his post to make sure he didn't spot Blizzard or Little Bighorn escaping.

Kaleena tapped her friend, then pointed to a security camera mounted high on a pole. With a nod, Jordynn headed over to it. The lens stared down at her like the shiny black eye of a robot. She momentarily opened her right pocket and allowed half of her chameleons to crawl inside. The remaining chameleons scattered along her body, but were unable to fully camouflage her. She remained partly visible, a ghostly girl with a thick Afro.

Jordynn took a deep breath. Then she stared into the robot eye on the camera and began to wave her arms back and forth.

CHAPTER 29

THE CROC CRATER

Noah leaned his forehead on the glass and stared down into the Croc Crater. Perhaps thirty feet beneath him, Tank and the three Descenders were spread out across a dirt floor with patches of tall yellow grass. Around them, trees rose and weak waterfalls trickled. Two walls of the pit resembled the walls of a rocky mountainside.

Tameron looked worse off than the others. He lay with his head in Hannah's lap. His eyes and mouth were half open, and Hannah was fanning his face with her hand. Sam and Tank were both sitting with their backs against a concrete wall, their heads slumped onto their raised knees.

"I'm sending them," Evie whispered, and then Noah heard one of her portal pockets unzip. Dozens of chameleons streamed up her leg, across her torso, and then up her arm and onto the trunk of a nearby tree. From there, they scurried along a branch and dropped on the glass roof of the enclosure. Evie grabbed the last chameleon before it got too far and attached a folded piece of paper to its back with a rubber band. Then she sent the chameleon on its way.

The chameleons wiggled through air vents, landing in the treetops. From there, they crawled along the branches, down the trunks, and onto the ground, where they headed for the people they had come to rescue.

When Tank noticed a chameleon crawling on his leg, he raised his hand to swat it, and then stopped his arm in mid-swing.

Sam's muffled voice came through the glass: "Tank! What's happening?" Noah saw that the chameleons were ghosting him.

Tank looked up and spotted the chameleons streaming down the tree trunk. Then Noah heard his voice: "It's them."

Hannah and Tameron, Noah saw, were also disappearing beneath the chameleon's magic.

Tank scooped up the chameleon with the message, pulled off the rubber band, and smoothed the page.

"What does it say?" Noah asked Evie.

"'Get Charlie's attention.'"

Tank stood, his body beginning to disappear. Then he turned his face toward the heights, and hollered as loud as he could: *"Rrraaahhh!"* His scream carried cleanly through the vents and out into the Creepy Core.

Within seconds, Charlie Red appeared in the open, torch-lit doorway to the side room, his hair a wild shock of red, his giant freckles spotting his face. He dashed toward the Croc Crater, flattening a few bugs on the way, and then pressed his face against the glass. Peering down, he slid along the glass, moving his head again and again because he couldn't believe what he saw, which was nothing. His prisoners were gone, or so it seemed. Swearing, Charlie banged a fist on the glass. Then he turned and ran toward the door marked "Lower Level."

"Let's go," Evie whispered to Noah and Ella, and the three of them took off running.

When Charlie pulled back the door, insects were dragged along the floor and heaped into a pile. Evie and the scouts followed on his heels. They quietly pursued him down a curving flight of stairs, Charlie's footsteps echoing in the hard, hollow space, and then followed him out into a narrow hallway that extended in both directions. Charlie headed left, wound around a curve, and then stopped at a door marked, "Croc Crater." He peered into the room through a small window.

He cursed again, then unsnapped a key chain from his hip and fumbled with it, the ring and clatter startling a group of spiders. Just as he was about to open the door, he froze and stared through the window, seeming suddenly concerned. Noah willed him to go inside, but he didn't, and worse, he reached for his walkie-talkie.

But before he could press the button to talk, his head suddenly rocked forward and clunked against the window—Evie's work, no doubt. His limp body collapsed in a heap, and then Evie dragged him out of the way to pry open the door.

"Evie?" someone inside the room said, and Noah realized it had been Tank.

"It's me. I got Noah and Ella with me."

"Guys—let's go!" Tank said. After a few seconds, Charlie's legs lifted up by his ankles and then he was dragged into the room.

"Check him for a headset," Evie said. "And get rid of his walkie-talkie."

Charlie's head turned one way, and then the other— Tank was checking his ears. Then his walkie-talkie rose off his hip and smashed to pieces against the floor. A second later, Noah felt Tank brush by him, and then Evie locked the door.

Together, the seven of them escaped up the stairs and

gathered in the Creepy Core. One of the Descenders started to groan.

"Shh . . ." someone softly said, and Noah realized it had been Hannah. "Tameron—he's in a bad way," she explained. "We're holding him up—me and Tank."

Noah heard the rip of a zipper, and then Evie said, "Here." A pair of boots appeared, and then two leather jackets. Evie handed off the gear, which seemed to float and bob as the Descenders dressed in it. The chameleons quickly made everything disappear.

"What about Tameron's pack?" Ella whispered.

"Keep it on," Evie said. "And keep it safe."

"You got a plan to get out of here?" Tank asked.

"We got a path," Evie answered. "We saw sasquatches on the way, maybe ten, maybe more. Follow my voice. If I can't talk, I'll mark myself. Eight corridors to the front door. Keep quiet and close. One corridor is full of snakes. Once we get beyond that, everything should be easier."

"*Should* . . . or *will*?" Tank asked.

Instead of answering, Evie said, "Let's go."

CHAPTER 30
DeGRAFF'S ORDERS

Jonathan DeGraff moved through the corridors on his way to the Creepy Core. A komodo dragon—or what had once been a komodo dragon, the lizard now sick with the Shadowist's magic and looking more monstrous than ever—was following at his feet, its long tail sweeping aside insects and the glass shards of broken aquariums.

At Legless Lane, DeGraff abruptly stopped when he noticed a faint spot of light. He squatted and picked up a tiny electrical contraption shaped like a bug. The light at its core dimmed . . . and dimmed . . . and then blinked out. He pinched his fingers together and crushed it.

He stood and stared toward the Creepy Core, his hand clenched into a fist. It was them—the Secret Society had gotten in. Had Charlie Red activated the traps?

The darkness between him and the Creepy Core was deep enough for him to surge across, and he sucked back a deep breath, drew the magic of the shadows into his body, and felt himself dissipate. He focused on the end of Legless Lane, stepped forward, and felt an intense speed, as if he were being hurled through space. When his feet came down on the edge of the Creepy Core, the magic released his body all at once, his cells regrouping.

DeGraff surged next to the Croc Crater. He held his hands to one of the glass walls and peered into the pit. Inside was a single person, but not one of the prisoners. Charlie Red lay on the ground, his legs splayed.

The Shadowist slammed the side of his fist against the glass, causing the insects living inside of him to stir. Spindly legs brushed his dry lips as something climbed onto his tongue. He swallowed and felt the insect struggle to stay out of his throat. Then he touched his ear and pressed a button on the same type of headset the scouts and Descenders wore. "It's me."

A voice came through the speaker. "Mr. DeGraff?"

"We've been infiltrated. Activate the traps."

"Yes, sir."

"Mr. Red is down. I need you to alert everyone. Make

sure the sasquatches are at their posts. Our visitors have the prisoners, so they'll be trying to escape."

"Yes, Mr. DeGraff," the voice said.

DeGraff glanced over his shoulder at the sight of Charlie again. "Fool," he grumbled.

Then he turned to Legless Lane and used his magic to get across it in a single step.

CHAPTER 31

RICHIE RISES TO THE OCCASION

Richie was Lee-Lee's only hope.

The idea made Richie sick, but it also forced him to act. He needed to get the rhino away from the wading pool so he could safely pull Lee-Lee out. But how?

He glanced around the exhibit. The fake mountainside, the caves, the wall of steel bars. What could he do? Thinking of his nerd-gear, he reached into his pocket. His fingers closed on a pencil, a highlighter, a ruler, a penlight, a—

He went back to the penlight and pulled it out. Like the rest of Richie's belongings, it was invisible, but his thumb easily found the button to turn it on, and when a tiny beam of light sliced through the darkness, the rhino looked up. It grunt-snorted and took a few steps toward the near end of the pool, its stare locked on the light.

Richie's heart was hammering in his chest. His gaze moved from the rhino to Lee-Lee. Then he cocked his arm and hurled the penlight, which turned as it sailed through the air, its steady light streaking across the rocky-looking walls and grassy floor. It clinked against a concrete boulder and came to rest on the ground.

The rhino grunted and charged around the pool, its footfalls shaking the exhibit. Richie focused on the water and the wavering image of Lee-Lee. Then he realized he was running when he felt the ground moving beneath him. At the edge of the pool, he dove headfirst, mindful not to go deep. He felt Lee-Lee, wrapped his arms under her torso, and brought her to the surface. Then he waded across the pool and dragged her onto the shore.

"Lee-Lee!" he whispered urgently. "Get up! Wake up!" Her eyes were closed, but she seemed to be breathing.

From the corners of his eyes, Richie saw his penlight go out. He glanced up and realized the rhino had crushed it. Now the powerful animal was looking his way, and Richie realized Lee-Lee wasn't the only one who had had her chameleons stripped off. The rhino took a slow step, and then another.

Richie glanced over his shoulder. Just a few feet away was the wall of steel bars that protected visitors. When he saw that part of it was sectioned off into a door, he remembered Lee-Lee's magic key and unclipped it from her hip. Then he jumped to his feet and ran toward the back of the exhibit. Maybe he could open the door and lead the rhino through it—maybe lock the animal outside.

He stopped at the bars, and as he fumbled with the key, the rhino's footfalls grew louder and louder. Richie didn't dare look back. His hand steadied and the magic key slipped into the slot. He turned his wrist and heard the lock pop. With only seconds to get out of the way, he pushed through the door and dove out into the visitor area, over to one side. The charging rhino barreled through the doorway right behind him, and the entire building shook as it hurtled through.

Dazed, Richie forced himself to stand. The visitor area was perhaps two hundred feet long and twenty feet across. One wall consisted of the cage bars; the other was colorful brick. When he grabbed the steel door, trying to swing it shut and lock the angry rhino out of the cage where Lee-Lee still lay, it didn't budge, and he realized it was dangling at an angle, its top hinge broken and its bottom jammed against the ground.

The rhino snorted and swung around, and Richie took off running into the visitor area to keep the rhino's attention away from the helpless Lee-Lee. He ran past marble benches and tall ficus trees in weighty ceramic pots. The floor began to rumble, and he realized the rhino was bearing down on him again. As Richie dove off to one side, the animal charged past before coming to a quick halt.

He moved to the far side of a bench, putting it between him and the rhino, which paced forward, tiles cracking beneath its heavy hooves. A second later, it charged again. Richie jumped aside just as its snout flung the bench into the air, where it spun and crashed into the steel bars. The rhino turned and trampled a ficus tree, dirt spilling out and ceramic pieces clinking against the tiles.

Richie ran, uncertain about everything. A door stood in the far wall of the visitor area, but it was surely kept locked, and even if it wasn't, he couldn't lead the rhino outside.

As the ground began to tremble again, Richie lost his balance and fell.

THE BIZ WITH BLIZ

Megan stood frozen, watching the guard. The walkie-talkie hovered inches from his face. As his lips curled to form his first word, the black box shot out of his hand, struck the floor, and dropped its battery pack. The guard glanced at the suddenly distant walkie-talkie, then his hand. Before he could react, his head rocked to one side and he toppled over, banging against a wall of steel bars. He slipped to the ground and lay there in a knot of twisted limbs, unconscious.

Megan stared, dumbfounded.

A girl's voice came from beside the fallen guard, "Don't just stand there . . . *get your bear!*"

Megan realized what had happened. Sara. She'd slipped down the hall undetected and leveled the person who was about to radio in what he saw.

The guard's legs suddenly sprang feetfirst into the air. His body turned like a snake's, then he began to slide down the floor toward Megan, Sara dragging him by his ankles.

"C'mon!" Sara ordered. "Get Blizzard out so I can lock up this clown!"

The gate squealed as Megan shoved it all the way open.

Blizzard stood and nearly slipped on the straw-covered floor. Snarling, he took a nervous step to one side, his head hung low.

"Blizzard," Megan said, "it's me!"

The powerful polar bear let out a slow growl. His gaze was fixed on something toward the front of his cage, and when Megan looked over her shoulder, she realized what was wrong. It appeared that the guard was somehow sliding down the hall on his back.

Megan quickly opened one portal to send her chameleons back, but the noise of the zipper startled Blizzard more, and he charged for the open door, knocking her aside. The guard's legs dropped to the ground as Sara was struck, and then Blizzard plowed up the aisle. In seconds, he was gone.

"Get him!" Sara shouted.

Megan jumped to her feet and stumbled over the Specter after she headed out of the cage. She wondered why Sara wasn't following, and then realized she still needed to lock up the guard.

Megan heard a door bang open just before she turned in a new direction. Thirty feet away, Blizzard had charged out into the night, alone and afraid, and full of dangerous power.

CHAPTER 33

THE MONITORS, THE MIRAGE

Frank Redford stepped out the front door of the security building, jumped down the steps two at a time, then hurried across the sidewalk. In the fifteen years that he'd been a security guard at the Waterford Zoo, he'd never experienced a single break-in.

Until now.

Seconds ago, he'd seen someone standing near camera fourteen. A girl. A girl with tall, bushy hair. In the grainy, black-and-white monitor, she'd looked . . . strange. Ghostly, somehow.

Frank stripped the baton off his hip and moved into the

area that camera fourteen monitored. The girl wasn't there. He turned left, right. Was it possible that he'd imagined her in the video? She'd seemed so ghostly—could he say for certain that she'd actually been there? Maybe a spot had appeared on the screen, some type of interference or something. It sometimes happened with the old cameras. Maybe his tired eyes had imagined a person.

He looked all around a final time, then holstered his baton. Fifteen years with no break-ins—why was he being so jumpy?

As he turned to head back to his post, his security cap suddenly slipped off the back of his head. He spun around and saw it lying on the sidewalk, a dark oval among the shadows.

"What in the world . . ."

He looked around again. The only movement was the soft sway of tree branches. There was no one, especially no ghostly girl.

He swept up the cap by its brim and put it in its proper place. As he turned to go, his cap tipped forward, slipped across his face, and tumbled down his chest before landing flat on the ground.

He pulled his baton and spun around again, fully expecting to see the girl with the big hair. He turned left, right, left again. The baton trembled in his hand. Grumbling, he scooped up his hat and pulled it so far down on his head that his ears curled outward. He headed back to the security building—a bit quickly, he realized. When he got to the door and tried to turn the knob, it wouldn't budge. Locked. When he reached for the key chain on his hip, the familiar clink and rattle didn't come.

Frank Redford's keys were gone.

He cocked his baton again. No one was around. When he tried to ask, "Who's there?" the words wouldn't come because his breath was stuck in his throat.

He plucked his wallet from his jacket and opened it. Inside one of the leather pockets was an emergency key for the shack—all the guards carried one. Frank quickly pulled it out, jabbed it into the slot, and pushed his way inside, locking the dead bolt behind him, grateful that *this* lock only opened from the inside. Footsteps pounded up the outside stairs and then the door handle shook in his hand.

Someone was out there.

As Frank rushed over to get a walkie-talkie, his gaze happened upon the rows of monitors on the wall, and he saw something in camera nineteen that made him halt. A polar bear was charging across the open zoo yard. And in camera twenty-five, a rhino was out of its exhibit.

Frank flung open a steel cabinet and snatched a walkie-talkie off a shelf. He held it to his face and pressed a button.

"Adam—it's Frank."

He waited, the walkie-talkie trembling in his hand.

"Adam, come in!"

No answer. Something was wrong.

"Troy!" he said. "Pete! You there? I can't. . . ." His voice trailed off as he noticed the polar bear running past the zoo carousel.

A staticky voice came through the speaker. "Come back."

Frank realized the room was spinning, and he forced air in and out of his lungs. "Guys—we got . . ." He could hardly bring himself to say the words. "Two animals loose. A rhinoceros and a polar bear."

A chuckle came through the speaker. "No elephants? You sure camera twelve is clear?"

"Guys—I'm not joking! This is real!"

When the airwaves stayed quiet, Frank realized he was believed.

"I'm near the rhino exhibit," Pete said. "I can be there in five minutes."

"Copy that," Frank said. "Troy?"

"Where is it now? The bear, I mean."

"Near the carousel. I'm not picking him up on the cameras right now."

"I'm on my way."

Frank nodded, forgetting that no one could see him.

"Frank . . ." Troy said, "are these the animals the Clarksville Zoo brought us?"

"I don't know," Frank said, worried about the same thing. "They . . . they could be."

A pause, and then Troy's voice again, more serious than ever: "Frank—you better call the cops."

"Roger. I'll do that right now."

As he set down his walkie-talkie, he did a double take at the monitor for camera twenty-five. Someone was *in* the rhino exhibit. A kid—a kid with a red winter hat.

As Frank reached for the phone to dial 911, something crawled onto his desk. Some type of lizard—a chameleon. It was followed by another, and another, until dozens appeared.

Frank cursed under his breath. As he took a step back, he felt something pulling on his pants, and he looked down to see countless chameleons crawling up his legs. He screamed and swatted at them, again and again.

On the ground around him were hundreds of chameleons. Frank glanced toward the main door and realized they were coming through a mail slot.

He felt a tug on his jacket—the chameleons were past his waist now. He swatted a few away, but there were too many. They crawled onto his chest and over his shoulders, their claws pricking his bare neck. He looked down again and screamed at what he saw.

The chameleons were gone.

And so was his body.

Frank ran then. It was all he could think to do. He grabbed the door, pulled, and stepped onto the porch which, like his body, was no longer there even though he could feel it beneath him.

Nothing made sense anymore, and Frank continued to run. After a few seconds, his foot slipped on an icy patch and he fell. As he struggled to get up, he noticed his body was visible again, but now it was covered in long hair, like an animal's.

To his left, an administrative building was bathed in the light from a tall lamppost. Frank ran to one of its windows and stared into it, barely able to believe what he saw: the skin around his eyes and nose and mouth was black and leathery; he had deep, upturned nostrils and thin lips; and the rest of his head was covered in thick black hair.

Frank looked like an ape.

The world began to spin. Frank went hot, and then cold. He stopped moving, and then collapsed onto his back. The starry sky began to narrow and narrow, and beneath the sudden hum in his ears, he was able to make out two voices.

"At least we got this one," one said.

"Does it matter?" the other asked. "The damage is done."

The hum stopped, the starry sky disappeared, and Frank momentarily left the world, glad for it.

✤ CHAPTER 34 ✤

THE TRAP IN JELLY ALLEY

Noah followed Ella down a dark hall, occasionally reaching out to ensure she was still near. Though Noah couldn't see Tank and Hannah, he was certain that they were still helping Tameron along. Evie led them through a corridor, and then another, and then Fish Foyer appeared. As Noah stepped toward the intersection, one in which he knew Evie had turned right, he heard a loud rumbling in the dark corridor straight ahead and looked up to see three animals charge around a corner. A lion, a tiger, a rhinoceros—but with red eyes and bulging muscles. They looked monstrous, and Noah realized they'd been poisoned by DeGraff, just like the sasquatches and the monkeys that had invaded his room.

When Noah tried to run, he tripped on Ella and tumbled to the ground. He glanced up and saw the striped face of the tiger, the mangy mane of the lion, and the thick horn of the rhino, which was slicing through the vines dangling from above. The animals had already closed in.

Ella quickly reached under his arm and hoisted him up, but before Noah could get aside, something hooked his leg and he was hurled off his feet as the animals charged by. His head thumped the floor and stars streaked across his vision. He looked up: five yards now separated him from where he'd been standing. The rumble had stopped and the animals, who were behind Noah and Ella now, were turning around, their bodies colliding, their wide rumps smashing out a few aquariums. Noah sucked back a deep breath and kept perfectly still. The animals still couldn't see him, not with—

His thoughts stopped. On the floor, something was skittering toward him. A chameleon. He saw a second, a third, a fourth. As one stepped onto his hand, he realized he was visible. The chameleons had fallen off him when the animals had knocked him over.

Something soft and fluffy bumped against the side of

his face—one of Ella's earmuffs. She quickly helped him back to his feet, saying, *"C'mon, Noah! Stand!"*

As Noah took off running, the rumble of the animals started again. The floor began to quake and tremors carried up his legs. When the two scouts tried to turn down the corridor Evie and the others had taken, they were met with a steel wall which had somehow closed off their escape route. Noah, stunned, could hear someone pounding on the other side—Tank or one of the Descenders.

"This way!" Ella called out.

They tore off straight down the corridor with the mutated animals giving chase, their grunts and footfalls echoing off the hard glass walls. Remembering he was still visible, Noah unzipped his portal pocket, ordering a fresh batch of chameleons onto him. The two friends followed a bend and continued on, walls of aquariums blurring past and bugs crunching beneath their feet.

Noah glanced back and saw eyes glowing red in the dim light. The animals, he realized, were gaining ground on them.

"Go!" he commanded. *"Faster, faster!"*

They followed another turn and emerged in a new hall. Toward the end of it stood three figures—hulking, upright creatures that could only be sasquatches. A nearby torch made them glow orange. The sasquatches were blocking their escape.

Ella's screams echoed in the narrow space.

Noah realized he couldn't hear the rumble of the animals, and he glanced back to see that they'd come to a stop. Perhaps fifty yards divided the animals from the sasquatches, with the scouts somewhere in the middle.

"*Ella—stop!*" Noah said, and she did, so suddenly that Noah ran into her back.

"What are they doing?" she hollered.

Noah glanced up and down the hall. On one end, the sasquatches were standing side by side, their gargantuan shoulders touching, and on the other end, the animals were gathered, perfectly still.

"What are they waiting for?" Ella asked.

Steel walls suddenly sprang out from the walls on both sides of Noah and Ella, blocking off their attackers and confining the scouts to a space that was perhaps twenty yards long.

"*What's happening?*" Ella squealed.

The normal walls had rows and rows of intact aquariums full of colorful, glowing jellyfish. Along the corridor ceiling, stringy seaweed dangled, and Noah realized they were in the counterpart for the Clarksville Zoo's Jelly Alley.

Noah ran to one steel divider and slammed his shoulder against it. The wall didn't budge. As he rejoined Ella, glass shattered somewhere and she screamed. An aquarium along the bottom of one wall had broken and water was pouring into the sectioned-off corridor as if from a hole in a dam. The swirling flood quickly covered the floor and then rose past their ankles.

The scouts paced. Ella was muttering something under her breath, practically whimpering. The flood showed no signs of slowing, and Noah realized the broken aquarium connected to another place full of water—water that was being drained to Jelly Alley to drown the two of them.

Noah and Ella had fallen into one of DeGraff's traps.

CHAPTER 35

RICHIE AND THE RHINOS

The charging rhino was only a few feet away from Richie, its snout low, its horn aimed straight ahead. The floor quaked and shards of tile burst into the air. Just as Richie prepared for the worst, the rhino suddenly fell onto its side and slid past, its massive hooves just missing him. It crashed into a marble bench and ripped it from the floor. Standing in the rhino's former place was another, bigger rhinoceros, and Richie immediately recognized him. Little Bighorn.

Richie jumped to his feet and moved in behind his animal friend, and the floor shook as the other rhino got up. Little Bighorn stepped forward and came horn to horn with the rhino, which stood its ground for a few seconds and then slowly walked off, its head hung low. When it dared to glance back, Little Bighorn grunted and it quickly looked away.

With a breath of relief, Richie touched Little Bighorn's side and then quickly remembered Lee-Lee.

"C'mon!" he said, and he took off running.

Little Bighorn followed him into the cage, where Richie squatted beside the Specter, who was now on her hands and knees, her wet hair dangling around her face.

"You okay?"

Lee-Lee nodded and rose to her knees. Around her, a few chameleons were crawling in the wet dirt, their eyes shifting nervously. "He was in one of the caves," Lee-Lee said when she saw Little Bighorn standing behind him. "Asleep, I guess."

Richie nodded. As he stood, he helped Lee-Lee up. Then he patted Little Bighorn's side. "We got to go."

The huge rhinoceros understood what this meant, and he lowered himself to the ground. Richie climbed into the front spot on his back, and Lee-Lee took a seat behind him.

"Hold on to me," Richie said as Little Bighorn came to his feet, and Lee-Lee's arms wrapped around his stomach.

Little Bighorn trotted across the exhibit. At the rear

door, he abruptly stopped and perked up his ears. Richie heard something just beyond the exit. Soft crunches—feet coming down on crisp autumn leaves.

One of Lee-Lee's arms let go, and a second later Richie felt his portal pocket open and then the pad of tiny feet as dozens of chameleons streamed onto him and Little Bighorn. Parts of the rhino began to disappear—but was there time?

The crunching sound grew louder, and then the door flew open, revealing a security guard. His baton was raised, and he seemed ready to strike at anything. He came to a sudden stop and turned his head to listen to something.

Richie looked down at himself and Little Bighorn. Both were invisible.

The guard reached his other hand for his flashlight, decided against it, and stood with his elbow cocked out to his side like a cowboy at a showdown. Richie listened for what the guard could hear, and came up with nothing but the faint rustle of leaves and the weak drone of a faraway car.

The guard reached onto his hip and powered off his walkie-talkie. Then he tiptoed through the open door. He came within five feet of Little Bighorn—four feet, three feet, two.

Richie realized there was nothing he or Lee-Lee could

do to prevent what was about to happen, and a second later, the guard bumped into Little Bighorn's invisible snout and then let out a breathy grunt as he jumped back a few steps, his baton still cocked, his eyes as big and round as quarters. His eyes shifted left, then right. He raised his free arm, and as he eased his trembling fingertips forward, they brushed the rhino's horn, and a chameleon leaped onto the guard's hand and began to crawl across it, making it disappear.

Little Bighorn suddenly sneezed and a wet burst of air blew across the guard, peeling off his security hat and coating his face in snot. As the guard repeatedly blinked, Richie saw what he saw—the full face of a rhinoceros. The guard glanced down at his own chest, where strips of his body were now disappearing—a few chameleons had been flung off of Little Bighorn.

The guard dropped his walkie-talkie and ran outside. If he had stayed around a few seconds longer, he would have heard Richie say, *"Gesundheit!"* as Little Bighorn stomped out of Horns Aplenty, crushing the walkie-talkie on his way.

CHAPTER 36

ᛖEGAᚾ SᴑᴑᴛHES ᴛHE SAVAGE BEAST

Megan began to close in on Blizzard only because he'd stopped and was now staring down a security guard who had happened into his path. The guard, a man in his fifties, had big ears and a bushy mustache. His baton, which was raised above his head, was trembling with his arm. He reached for his walkie-talkie, dropped it, and either didn't realize it or care. Blizzard let out a low, slow growl, and slunk forward to within a few feet of him.

Megan remembered what the police officers had done to Blizzard in her school gym. He'd allowed himself to be captured because he'd believed he was protecting the

Secret Zoo. This time, however, things were different, and Megan realized the zoo guard was going to die if she didn't do something.

"*Blizzard! No!*" she hollered as she closed to within thirty feet of the scene.

Blizzard swung his long neck and glanced behind him. Seeing nothing, he turned back to the guard, whose baton was trembling more than ever.

"*Blizzard!*"

The bear turned his head again, and Megan hoped he knew her voice. As she closed to within ten feet, she opened her pocket and sent her chameleons away. Blizzard swung his body around and faced her, and after only a second or two, his tense muscles eased up.

"It's me!" she said. Then she wrapped her arms around Blizzard and pressed her face against his. Blizzard turned his snout and sniffed the air near her.

"I'm here to take you home," Megan said, and the thought of that softened her heart. Days ago, she'd never expected to see her polar bear friend again.

"What . . . what's going on?"

Megan peered over Blizzard to see the guard standing in the same place, his baton a shadowy back-and-forth blur above his head.

"Get back, kid!" the guard hollered.

Megan opened her pocket and disappeared again.

The man jumped to one side and then another, gazing everywhere.

"Over here," Megan said, and the guard spun around to where her voice was now coming from, several feet off to one side.

Megan glanced at Blizzard and was relieved to see he'd eased back a few steps and was no longer snarling.

"I'm here now," Megan said from the other side of the guard, who jumped and turned in the air, his worried eyes moving from spot to spot. "Drop the baton."

The guard did, next to his walkie-talkie.

As Megan picked both items up, they seemed to float in the air before disappearing in her camouflage.

Megan felt the air move beside her and realized Sara had joined them.

"Are you afraid?" Megan asked the guard.

The man nodded, again and again.

"Good. That'll keep you alive. I'm not alone, you know."

Megan elbowed Sara, who understood the cue. "If I were you, I'd do what she says."

The man gasped and jumped at the new voice. "Please . . . I have kids. A . . . a family."

"So do we," Megan said. "That's why we're here."

The guard nodded again.

"We're taking the bear. If you call the police in the next hour, we'll be back."

"I won't!" the man whimpered. "I promise!"

Megan grabbed Sara's wrist and led her over to Blizzard. She studied the bear's injuries and whispered, "Can you carry us?"

In answer, Blizzard lowered himself to the ground, and Megan and Sara climbed on, Megan in the front. Blizzard came to his feet—a bit slowly, Megan thought—and then trotted off. As he rounded a building, Megan heard a zipper opening and realized it was Sara's.

"Ghost him," Sara said.

Megan opened her pocket and allowed dozens of chameleons to portal through. They scattered across Blizzard's body and quickly camouflaged him. Megan smiled. Then she threw the guard's baton and walkie-talkie into a bush.

CHAPTER 37

THE JAM WITH THE JELLIES

It took only seconds for the water level to rise past their knees. Noah's pants clung to his body like thick skin. Something else was coming through the broken aquarium. Crabs. Dozens were riding the torrent, their claws reaching out, their back legs paddling futilely.

Noah waded though the flood, which was now at his waist, and fumbled along the walls, looking for some type of escape. He saw chameleons squirming in the growing depths and realized they were being stripped off him and Ella. Unable to stay afloat, the lizards plummeted toward the floor.

An idea struck him. The way the water was coming in could be their way out. He dove headfirst into the cold water, which stole his breath and what was left of his body heat. He paddled a sloppy breaststroke, his open eyes unable to focus on much. As he neared the broken aquarium, the flowing water pushed against him like an ocean wave, and after only a few seconds, he lost his strength and was sent backward. He surfaced, gasping for air, and found the flood was up to his chest now.

"What are you *doing*?" Ella said, and Noah realized she was visible again.

"The broken tank . . ." Noah panted. "I couldn't get through."

The flood reached Noah's neck, his chin, his mouth. He stood on his tiptoes, tipped back his head, and managed to keep his nose up for a few seconds. As the water continued to rise, he kicked his arms and legs and rose with it. Ella did the same.

A jellyfish floated by, the bell of its body opening and closing to guide it along. A second appeared, and then a third, a fourth. Some were clear, and others were tinted with vibrant reds and yellows and blues. Noah counted ten, fifteen, twenty. They were coming from the aquariums, the front walls of which were opening like glass doors—part of DeGraff's trap, no doubt. An entire bloom of jellyfish began to crowd the space around him, stringy tentacles dangling beneath bulbous bodies. Noah's clothes protected him from their sting, but he still dodged to keep them from touching his hands or his face.

As the flood rose higher and higher, the ceiling neared and sounds changed, echoes softening. The scouts fought the weight of their wet clothes to keep their heads up, and when the ceiling came to within three feet, its stringy seaweed stuck to Noah's cheeks. Finally, his head could go no further, and the water rose past his chin, his nose, his brow, and then claimed the last of the open space—the last of the Secret Jelly Alley's oxygen.

Noah swam down. With the torches out, the only light came from inside a few fish tanks. Hundreds of jellyfish seemed to be flying around him like bizarre birds from a planet in a dream. He felt a terrible sting and looked down to see a jellyfish touching his hand. Pressure built in his chest, and his heart began to hammer against his sternum. He needed air.

His gaze happened upon a dead chameleon floating by, its long, limp tail swaying in the currents, and Noah felt bad for it. The chameleon had so selflessly served the Specters and the Secret Society, always ready to portal from—

His thoughts stopped. The portal pockets—the Specters had told the scouts that anything could pass through them. And Noah had seen it happen with Richie's hand. Did "anything" include water?

Noah didn't waste any more time wondering. He reached down, unzipped his right pocket, and immediately felt water flow through the opening. His limbs were pushed and pulled by a swirl of different currents.

Ella saw what was happening and followed his lead. The water level began to fall, and the ceiling of Jelly Alley seemed to rise into the air, water dripping from its green seaweed. The scouts surfaced and greedily sucked back several breaths.

Noah felt his stomach burning, and when he dunked his head, he saw a jellyfish had gotten under his shirt. He tried to flick it off, noticing more jellyfish on his pants. As several crabs neared, he used his arm to bat them away. The water wasn't the only thing being sucked toward his pocket.

The scouts were lowered farther and farther from the ceiling, and then finally touched the floor. The water had stopped gushing from the broken aquarium, leaving a pool that stopped at the height of their pockets. Jellyfish and crabs were floating all around.

"I can't believe. . . ." Ella gazed at her arms, her hands, her stomach. "I can't believe we're not *dead*." She touched his palms to her wet earmuffs, as if to ensure her head was still there. "I mean . . . we're not, right?"

"Not yet," Noah said. "What do you think happened to all the chameleons at the Portal Place?"

Ella shrugged. "Probably got flushed out of their build-ing." She jumped to one side to avoid a crab. "We better come up with a plan to get out of here pretty fast."

Noah remembered his idea from earlier. "We can make it out through the aquarium, the one all this water came from." He waded to one side of the corri-dor, avoiding jellyfish. "C'mon—this way." When they reached the wall, he stuck his foot through the hole in an aquarium near the floor, saying, "This is the one—the big rectangular one."

Ella said, "But what if it connects to a tunnel . . . like in the Grottoes? How long will we need to hold our breath?"

Noah ignored the question and moved his leg to force a few crabs aside. Then he shook out his shoulders. "Let's go."

When he plunged headfirst into the open aquarium, Ella followed.

CHAPTER 38

ESCAPE FROM WATERFORD ZOO

"Head to the far side of the zoo," Megan said, "toward the water tower."

Blizzard grunted and broke into a run. As his muscles quaked, so did Megan's, and the chameleons poked her as they struggled to hold on.

They rounded a fountain with statues of several seals pointing their slender snouts toward the sky, then turned onto a long brick walkway. A camel exhibit blurred by, and then an empty gorilla yard. Through Blizzard's invisible body, Megan watched the powdery snow swirl.

As Blizzard veered back onto a long stretch of grass,

she sensed something beside her, and under the drum of Blizzard's steps, she heard a low rumble—another animal on the run.

Sara said, "Lee-Lee—that you?"

"Roger that, girl," a voice beside Megan answered.

Something snorted and blew snot into the air. Little Big.

"Richie?" Megan said. "You there?"

"I'm here," Richie answered, his voice jittering.

Together, the two animals circled a glass butterfly house, and then veered past a brick building covered in a leafless web of ivy. As they ran across a garden, Blizzard left a three-foot-high flowerpot spinning like a top. At an outdoor food court, they toppled tables and knocked benches into the air. Closed umbrellas twirled like giant batons, and crumpled napkins and half-eaten hamburgers exploded from garbage cans.

As they headed back onto a main path, Megan heard a zipper open and turned to see a stack of paper spreading out behind Little Bighorn like the watery wake behind a speedboat. The flyers stuck to the sides of buildings, became entwined in bushes, and covered parts of the yard like fresh snow. In her head, Megan could see their words: "Free them or we will!"

The winding chain-link fence came into view, moonlight glinting on the diamond patterns of its woven wire.

Their truck was still parked in the small gravel lot, its big door open and waiting. As Blizzard neared it, Sara said, "Duck!" and Megan pressed her forehead against the bear's neck. She heard the rattle of flimsy steel, then a light piece of fencing skipped across her back. Blizzard pounded up the loading ramp into the trailer, and as he swung around in the hollow space, Megan saw what he'd done to the fence: a large steel piece was dangling off to one side, and an uprooted post was aimed at an angle toward the night sky like a telescope.

The truck continued to bounce and rattle on its springs as Little Bighorn made his way into the trailer. Megan slid down Blizzard's side and felt Sara do the same.

"Everyone okay?" someone asked, and Megan turned to see Solana.

"I think so," Megan said.

The benches rattled as the girls and Richie dropped into their former seats. They stayed invisible while waiting for the other Specters to arrive. Megan stared out through the open loading door at a few distant houses and couldn't detect any activity.

A minute went by. Then another. Just when Megan worried that something might have happened to Kaleena and Jordynn, footsteps sounded against the loading ramp and the presence of the remaining Specters became obvious inside the trailer.

With everyone accounted for, Sara rapped her knuckles against the forward wall of the trailer. The driver door creaked open and then gravel crunched as Mike made his way to the back of the truck. He reached up, grabbed the nylon strap, and pulled the door closed, delivering the girls and Richie into perfect darkness.

As the truck pulled off onto the street, someone turned on the overhead lights. Megan opened the portal in her right pocket when she heard other Specters doing it. Within seconds, the chameleons were gone and everyone, including Blizzard and Little Bighorn, was visible once more.

Blizzard carefully lowered himself to his stomach and shifted his rump to one side to keep the weight off his injured leg. One of his patches of gauze was saturated in blood, the wound fresh again after his strenuous run. He rested his chin on his outstretched legs and half closed his eyes, his sides heaving up and down.

Megan slid down her seat, leaned over, and lovingly stroked the top of Blizzard's long neck, prompting the bear to completely close his eyes.

Sara turned to Blizzard. She crossed her arms over her chest and shook her head, clearly disgusted by what had happened to him.

"What do you think they'll do?" Solana asked out of the blue.

Sara turned her head and realized Solana was speaking to her. "Who?"

"The Outsiders," Solana clarified. "When they find the flyers—what do you think they'll do?"

Sara slouched in her chair and kicked her legs out straight. She grunted and said, "I could care less."

Megan turned to Richie and briefly squeezed his hand. Then she tipped her head back against the wall, closed her eyes, and wondered about Noah and her best friend.

CHAPTER 39

THE CRABAQUARIUM

Noah swam into the aquarium, dim light revealing that a dark tunnel extended from the back of it. He found his way by patting the concrete walls around him. Something slimy struck his face, and he hoped it had been seaweed rather than the stinging tentacle of a jellyfish. Something pinched his pants—a crab. Noah dragged it along.

He needed air. He spotted a wavering point of light and swam to it with all his strength. Not a second too soon, he surfaced and sucked in a quick breath. He found himself waist deep in an aquarium that was easily a hundred feet long. One side, as big as a movie screen, was made of glass, and Noah looked out into a corridor that was like the others he'd seen.

As Ella surfaced beside him, another crab pinched his leg. Dozens of others were paddling around in the shallow water.

"Crabaquarium," he breathed.

Another crab pinched him, this time breaking through to his flesh, and Noah batted it away with the back of his hand. He looked around for an exit and couldn't find one. Then he walked to the front of the aquarium, put his hands on the glass, and pushed. The pane didn't budge. "There's no way out of here."

Ella swiped her arm through the water at a crab that was getting too close. "Maybe we should go back."

Before Noah could respond, a small steel door dropped across the mouth of the tunnel that they'd swum through. Then, from down the corridor, a shadowy figure came walking. A single torch revealed a man with a fedora hat and a long, flowing trench coat.

DeGraff.

↬ CHAPTER 40 ↫

THE SHADOWS

The Shadowist walked down the corridor, his face concealed by the brim of his hat. He stopped in front of the scouts, less than ten feet away, and stood with his hands clasped behind his back. For what seemed a long time, he didn't move. Then he walked forward and stopped less than a foot from the glass.

The scouts crowded against the back wall of the Secret Crabaquarium, Ella with her arms around Noah. The crabs continued to swim around, pinching at their legs.

"What do you want!" Noah yelled.

DeGraff only tipped his head to one side in a casual,

curious way, as if he weren't staring into an aquarium full of kids, but one with fish. He reached up a gloved hand and stroked his shadowy chin. Then he touched his palm to the glass and drummed his fingers against it.

"He can't . . . he can't get us, can he?" Ella softly spoke.

DeGraff moved his head for a better look at them and subsequently revealed his face—or what was left of it. For the first time, Ella saw the dark skull cavities where DeGraff's eyes and nose should have been; the flesh missing above his top teeth; the gash exposing his jaw. The skin on his neck bubbled out as an insect crawled beneath it. He turned and walked slowly to the middle of the corridor, its only torch at his back. His shadow was stretched out across the floor in front of him, onto the tank, and across the water beside the scouts. Beneath it, several crabs were thrashing about, their claws striking out at nothing.

But DeGraff's interest, Noah knew, wasn't in the crabs— it was in him and Ella. And just as he had this thought, DeGraff began to walk down the corridor, easing his shadow toward them. Noah noticed the silhouette of his fedora moving across the stony back wall of Crabaquarium.

"His shadow!" Noah called out. *"Move, move!"*

Ella understood at once, and together they splashed toward the other end of the aquarium. They passed cleanly through DeGraff's shadow, Noah feeling a twinge of its magic in the short time. DeGraff began to follow them, bringing his shadow along.

"Keep going!" Noah said.

Ella dove forward, swimming with wild, careless strokes. Noah stopped and faced the corridor, his palms against the glass.

"Right here, you *freak!*" Noah screamed, trying to lure the Shadowist away from his friend.

DeGraff's shadow slithered across the water like a living thing. Then it cloaked Noah, who gazed down at his arms, his chest. Nothing was happening. But just as he had this thought, the right side of his body jerked. A second later, his left side spasmed, and then his right again. Pain shot through him, and noises dimmed beneath a high-pitched squeal.

"*Noah—no!*" someone called out. Noah wondered who it had been. Richie? No, it had sounded like a girl. He tried to think of his sister's name and couldn't. His head—something was wrong.

His arms thrashed and Noah twisted to face the back of the aquarium. He saw DeGraff's shadow on the wall—it had become one with his, the fedora seeming to sit on Noah's head.

Then Noah lost sight of the world as his eyes rolled back. His knees gave out and he slumped to one side, sinking into the water. Powerless to raise his head, Noah became certain this was the place he was going to die.

CHAPTER 41

ELLA TAKES A SWING

Ella splashed over to Noah, calling his name.

"Up, Noah! Get up!"

As she struggled through the water, one strap of Tameron's pack slipped off her shoulder and caught in the crook of her arm. She returned it to its former spot, cursing the pack, which had been good for nothing. Only Tameron could—

A thought grabbed her. *Was* Tameron the only person who could use the backpack? Or could anyone? Could *she*?

She remembered back to the times she'd seen Tameron

decked out in his Descender gear. Had she ever noticed what he did to join the tail to his body? No, but Sam opened zippers on his jacket to release his wings, and Hannah tugged pull-loops to alter her boots.

She looked at the backpack straps and noticed that, near her shoulders, two cords disappeared into holes circled by velvet patches. She grabbed one in each hand, and then hesitated. But somewhere beneath the choppy water, Noah was thrashing about, drowning in DeGraff's power.

She pulled the cords. Two clicks sounded inside the pack, and then a great weight dropped from her shoulders. Something had fallen out, and she was certain what it was.

Tameron's tail.

One end seemed to grab on to the base of her spine, and brief pain shot through her body. Her mind sparked, and she suddenly became aware of her tailbone—the muscles there. She peered over her shoulder to see the long appendage half floating in the water. The canvas pack was somehow fused into the back of Ella's shirt, which now looked like the armored plate of an animal.

Ella put all her attention on the tail and tried to make it move. It immediately rose like a serpent, water pouring off its sides. Then it hovered several feet in the air.

Fifteen feet long, its armor was studded with spikes, most of them at the tip.

Without wasting another second, Ella turned in a circle and commanded the tail to swing with all its might. The monstrous appendage flew through the air, and when it struck the front of the aquarium, the wall shattered, sending a spray of glass at DeGraff, who ducked and covered his head. Hundreds of gallons of water spilled out, and the small tidal wave knocked DeGraff down and pushed him against the wall. The scouts washed out into the corridor.

It took only seconds for the flood to subside. Ella ran across the wet floor to Noah, her tail sweeping up pieces of broken glass, and fell to her knees beside her friend. As she heaved him up by his shoulders, his eyes rolled back into his head.

"Noah!" she said, and then shook him.

She noticed that DeGraff was slowly rising to his feet, and she slapped Noah across his face, hard. His eyes turned, and his oversized pupils shrank in the flickering torch light. He coughed and water dribbled down his chin.

Ella looked back and saw the Shadowist standing. He straightened his fedora and then advanced on the scouts, his boots splashing on the wet stone. She rose and turned to face him, her tail curling behind her.

"What are you doing?" Noah managed to say.

But Ella didn't respond. She simply stepped toward DeGraff, whipping around Tameron's tail and bringing his mighty power as a Descender with her.

CHAPTER 42

ELLA VERSUS DEGRAFF

As Ella moved in on the Shadowist, she saw glass fragments embedded in his cheeks and neck, black blood oozing from the wounds. Tameron's tail pulled on her spine as it dragged across the floor. She swung her body just as she had in the Crabaquarium, and the tail came off the ground and flew through the air, its pointed tip dragging along the far wall, shattering aquariums and batting chunks of stone all around. As it reached DeGraff, he disappeared into the shadows just long enough for it to pass, and then reappeared in the same spot, a mirthless smile spreading on his face. Ella reversed the swing of her hips and the tail whipped in the opposite direction. DeGraff vanished into the shadows a second time and the tail crashed into the wall, the spikes on its tip becoming ensnarled in the framework of a broken aquarium. Ella yanked once, twice, and then the wall burst open, raining pieces of stone and glass into the corridor. Her tail bounced off the ground.

DeGraff gave a grunt that might have been a laugh, and said, "Child—do you honestly believe you can defeat me?" He plucked a shard of glass from his face and flicked it into the air. "Try again?"

Ella flung the tail high over her head. The powerful appendage dragged along the ceiling and came down toward DeGraff, who disappeared into the shadows again. The tail smashed into the floor, pieces of stone exploding in a cloud of dust.

A voice came from behind her: "Over here, girl."

Ella spun as hard as she could. The tail whipped around, its tip passing through the open wall of the Crabaquarium, and whooshed through the air, missing DeGraff as he dissolved into the shadows again.

Laughter came from behind her, and Ella turned, this time without attacking. DeGraff stood several feet away from her, his body cloaked in shadow.

"Now . . . my turn," he said.

Before she could think to respond, DeGraff disappeared,

and then Ella felt two tugs on the cords of her shoulder straps—he was behind her. Pain surged through her spine and then Tameron's tail was coiled inside its pack again. She was jolted around as DeGraff stripped the pack off her shoulders. It flew out over her head, struck the ground, and slid to a stop twenty feet away. Then Ella's head rocked as DeGraff threw her to the cold floor. She turned onto her back and stared up at the Shadowist, who now loomed above her.

DeGraff said, "It's time to—"

Something struck his face. He reached up, pulling away a wet, jellylike substance, and then let loose a deep, visceral scream, partly in anger, partly in pain.

Ella looked behind her and understood what had happened. Noah. On his knees, he was flicking his wrist, trying to get something off his hand. The substance: jellyfish.

DeGraff rubbed at his face and staggered to one side of the corridor.

Ella jumped to her feet and ran over to Noah. "Up!" she commanded as she reached under his arms and lifted. *"Get up!"* She grabbed Tameron's gear and hoisted it onto her back. Then she ran with Noah, her arm under his for support.

They rounded a bend and saw that the corridor came to a sudden end at an open doorway. The scouts rushed through it, having no idea where it might lead.

CHAPTER 43

THE SECRET CHAMBER OF LIGHTS

Noah concentrated on matching Ella's pace as they rushed down a winding glass tunnel surrounded by water filled with hundreds of blinking white lights. Flashlight fish, Noah realized—tiny animals that could emit spots of light. There were so many that it felt like the scouts had discovered a passage into a magical night sky. Noah had no doubt that they were in the Secret Zoo's version of the Clarksville Zoo's Chamber of Lights.

"Faster!" Ella said to Noah. "You're slowing down!" As they neared a bend in the tunnel, Ella looked back and gasped, "He's coming!"

Noah glanced over his shoulder to see DeGraff stepping into the tunnel. He was staggering a bit, still wiping the jellyfish from his face. The light from the flashlight fish made different parts of him pulse in and out of view. The folds of his jacket. The buckles in his boots. The sharp edge of his collar.

Noah lost his balance and dropped to one knee. As Ella helped him up, hundreds of flashlight fish streaked across his vision like sparklers being waved on a summer night. Then he ran forward again, still groggy.

The scouts charged around another bend, and then another. Noah heard the thuds of DeGraff's black boots, and he knew it would only take seconds for him to overtake the scouts.

The end of the corridor came into view, an open doorway into a dark space. Noah lost his balance, staggered in front of Ella, and the two collided and tumbled to the floor. Noah forced himself up to his hands and knees, and looked to see DeGraff less than twenty feet away.

A blinding pulse of light forced his eyes closed. It was so powerful that Noah couldn't hide from it—his eyelids lit the same way a window shade does in the morning sun.

"What's *happening?*" Ella screamed.

A wail of pain canceled all other sound. DeGraff was

standing above Noah, and something was wrong with him.

Noah waited a few seconds and then peeled back one eyelid. When light blinded him, he closed it again.

DeGraff continued to howl, and the floor shook as he staggered.

Noah waited some more and then forced his eyes to open and stay that way. All he could see was a flat, dimensionless white. He realized DeGraff's painful wail was no longer coming from above him; it was coming from beside him.

The world slowly came into focus. Three feet over to Noah's left, DeGraff was on his knees, his back hunched, his head down. His trench coat was draped over him, and the leathery mound of his body reminded Noah of a turtle tucked into its shell. The area around him was such a stark white that Noah couldn't see a suggestion of anything else. The winding tunnel walls, the fish—all of it was gone.

DeGraff's scream subsided, then stopped altogether. As he huddled beneath his trench coat, Noah understood why. This shadowless world was hurting him.

Noah rose to his knees and looked around. Ella was on her feet beside him, her eyes shut tight.

"It's safe!" Noah said. "It's okay to look!"

Ella slowly peered out. "Wha—? Where are we? Did we

portal?" She paused for a few seconds, then added, "Oh, no . . . we've gone amiss!"

Noah shook his head. "How? We didn't go through a gateway."

He reached up and touched something smooth and cold. Glass.

"The wall," he said as he slid his hand along. "The tunnel . . . it's still here."

"But . . . but how?" Ella asked. "Where did—"

"The flashlight fish," Noah interrupted. "They're causing this."

Noah recalled when the flashlight fish had shined their magical light during a power outage at the Clarksville Zoo. He looked at DeGraff, on the ground, his trench coat draped across his body, and realized the fish were still on the scouts' side.

"Let's go," Ella said. She pointed to the end of the corridor, where an open doorway stood, and then moved in beside Noah to support him again. "You okay?"

Noah felt nauseated, but no longer dizzy. He gave a quick nod.

Together, they headed up the bright corridor. "Just keep holding me," Ella said. "Don't let go."

Noah glanced back. DeGraff had begun to crawl after them, his face tucked beneath a flap of his trench coat. The coat and hat—they protected him by keeping him in constant shadow, Noah realized. DeGraff's wardrobe kept him alive when he was in the light.

"Hurry!" Noah said. "He's coming!"

The two of them located the open doorway and escaped from the blinding light.

☙ CHAPTER 44 ❧

THE CORRIDOR OF PORTALS

The corridor outside the Chamber of Lights was like most of the others: a stone floor, aquariums set in the walls, and green slime dripping from the ceiling. Insects covered everything. The passage ran to the left and right of where the scouts were standing.

"Which way?" Ella asked.

Noah shrugged. "I don't know, but we should ghost."

Ella quickly unzipped her portal pocket. When no chameleons came out, Noah opened his and got the same result.

"They're not there," Ella said. "The water—it must have washed them out of the Portal Place."

From the dark distance, something flew toward them, and the light from a torch revealed a tiny blue bird with a big beak. Marlo. The kingfisher touched down on Noah's shoulder, chirped once, and then flew back the way he'd come.

"Let's go," Ella said.

As they followed Marlo, Noah no longer needed Ella's support. The two of them ran down the corridor, turned left, then hurried down another. Every time Marlo got too far ahead, he found a perch and waited. They headed down a third corridor, a fourth, a fifth. Big black ants covered the floor of one passage, and the scouts ran on their tiptoes, trying not to hear their bodies crunch.

In a particularly dark corridor, Marlo flew back and landed on Noah, chirping wildly.

"What is it?" Ella asked.

From up ahead came a deep, rumbling growl. Noah thought he could hear the click of hooves and the thump of padded paws.

"Ours or DeGraff's?" Ella asked.

Noah knew they couldn't just stand there waiting to find out. A few steps ahead, an open doorway led to a dark space clouded with fog. A sign by the door read, "The Corridor of Portals." Noah pointed to it.

"The Corridor of Portals?" Ella said.

Noah understood her confusion. There was no Corridor of Portals in the Clarksville Zoo.

The rumble of the animals grew louder. New sounds took shape: the grunt of a rhinoceros, a rumbling growl.

"C'mon!" Noah said.

They ran forward and ducked through the doorway. A few steps away, the new corridor became a steep, sloping tunnel with dirt walls and a muddy floor.

Ella stepped onto the slope and immediately lost her footing. She dropped to her rear end and sailed down, as if on a slide. Noah followed. They landed in a heap where the cave floor went flat and quickly untangled themselves. On their stomachs, they stared up the incline, which had a partial view into the hall above. Marlo had landed again on Noah's shoulder and was keeping perfectly still, his bright orange bill tipped toward the doorway above.

The noise grew louder, and distinct sounds continued to take shape. The cave walls began to tremble, and clumps of dirt rained down from the ceiling. Bugs scattered to new spots. Marlo gave a weak, frightened chirp and stepped closer to Noah's neck.

As rhinos and tigers charged past the entrance to the Corridor of Portals, Noah saw their red eyes and long, filthy hair. Within seconds, the walls stopped shuddering and the noises died.

"They're gone," Noah said. "C'mon, let's—" His voice stopped as he happened to glance over his shoulder.

When Ella saw what Noah was looking at, she gasped. Across the muddy floor of the foggy cave, puddles sat in the craterlike footprints of sasquatches. Along the walls, dozens of dark openings gave way to new places. Caves. To Noah, it looked like they'd been dug out by the same sasquatches that had left the footprints.

Noah crouched down and touched the mud, which oozed over his fingertips, releasing a foul, earthy odor. Marlo chirped nervously and hopped to a new spot on his shoulder.

"Noah?" Ella said. "Yeah . . . I'm thinking *right now* would be a good time to get out of here."

Noah flicked the wet earth off his hand and gazed down the cave. "What's DeGraff doing down here?" He rose and took a step forward, Marlo jumping on his shoulder and chirping in protest. Noah noticed how words were engraved in the packed dirt above the mouths of the caves.

"Ella . . ." he said, and he pointed to the place above the first entrance.

"'Forest of Flight,'" she read.

Noah read the words above the next cave: "'A-Lotta-Hippopotami.'"

"He's creating new portals," Ella said. "So he doesn't have to use the ones that we do."

Noah shuddered as he saw the words marking the third tunnel: "Nowicki House." Marlo gave another worried chirp and stepped back and forth, restlessly.

"This was the one . . ." Noah said. "To my closet."

Ella nodded. "How many others go beyond the Clarksville Zoo?"

Noah shrugged and continued to read the engravings. The forth cave was marked "Rhinorama," and the fifth was marked "Clarksville Elementary." He tried to read the words above the sixth and couldn't—the fog was too thick, the tunnel too dark. As he took a step nearer, Marlo chirped his disapproval.

"Relax," Noah said to his kingfisher friend. "I just want to see."

He took another step, and then a third. He could make out the bottom word: "Giza." He'd heard "Giza" before, but where?

Something poked his rear end, and he spun around. Marlo had jumped off his shoulder and jabbed him with his beak. Now the kingfisher was flying through the fog back toward the muddy incline. He found a perch on the bumpy wall and chirped. His message was clear—he wanted everyone out of the Corridor of Portals.

"He's right," Ella said. "DeGraff—he could already be on our trail again."

Noah glanced at the cave marked "Giza" and made out the word "of" above it.

" 'Of Giza . . .' " Noah said. "Why is that so—?"

"C'mon, already!" Ella insisted.

Noah turned and fled.

CHAPTER 45

BACK AT POCKETS OF PORTALS

Outside City Treats and Sector Sweets, what was left of a flood of water was dripping through the sewer grates. Jellyfish lay across the sidewalks, and a few crabs were crawling about.

The chameleons began to make their way back to the old bakery—a few at first, then more and more. They crawled across the wet threshold and splashed through puddles, a thousand eyes turning in all directions.

They headed through a door at the back of the building and stopped at the storage room, where the racks were still wet. Jellyfish lay across countertops, wrapped around the legs of chairs, and clung to the fabric of old aprons. A few dripped like snot from the rails of the racks. Beneath some of them, chameleons lay dead, victims of their stings.

The chameleons moved into the room and began to clamber up the racks to their posts, committed as always to serving the Specters and the Secret Zoo.

❧ CHAPTER 46 ❧

THE MIRAGE

Marlo led them down several winding corridors which the scouts hadn't seen before. In one, they had to duck into a dark corner to avoid being spotted by a pair of sasquatches. In another, beetles cracked and crunched like fortune cookies beneath their feet. As they turned into the long corridor leading to the City of Species, Noah realized that a torch was now burning and all the sasquatches were gone. Seconds later, he heard something behind them—the thump of boot heels and the flap and clap of long leather. DeGraff.

Noah and Ella picked up speed, bugs scattering at their

feet. The gateway neared to within forty feet, thirty feet, twenty feet. Noah felt something moving on his stomach and looked down to see a few wet chameleons crawling out of his portal pocket, which he must have left open. In the Streets of Transparency, something must have changed.

As Marlo flew between the curtains and was gone, Noah wondered who was gathered around the portal. The Descenders, for sure, and certainly Mr. Darby. Just as Ella was about to take her turn, Noah suddenly had an idea and pulled her back.

"Go without me!" he said.

"*What?* What are you—"

"Tell Mr. Darby I'm sending DeGraff."

"Are you out of your *mind*?"

"*Just do it!*" Noah said. "Trust me. Mr. Darby will be there—tell him to get ready."

Ella hesitated, then turned and disappeared into the City of Species without another word.

More and more chameleons were portaling through his pocket now, some crawling up Noah's body and others falling to the floor. Once at least fifty were out, he closed his zipper and backed up against the wall beside the velvet curtains, hoping the chameleons would understand his intentions.

"*C'mon,*" he breathed. "*Work, work. . . .*"

He concentrated on what he wanted the lizards to do. Evie had been able to make herself look like Richie—a *mirage*, she had called it. "We think, they do," she'd said. Maybe Noah could create an illusion as well, and make the portal to the City of Species vanish.

The chameleons began to crawl onto the footholds in the stony wall and cling to folds of the curtains. As they spread out, Noah imagined what the corridor would look like if it didn't end. Just a continuing stretch of darkness. More torches burning. More bugs scuttling and scrambling and flying.

Seconds passed. Noah thought harder and harder, and tried to ignore DeGraff's footfalls, which were louder than ever. Just when he worried that nothing would happen, he felt pressure just behind his forehead, and the chameleons came into extraordinary focus. He could plainly see their details—their colorful stripes, their bumpy skin, their bulbous eyes. And somehow, he could feel them. They suddenly seemed like extensions of himself, things he could control as easily as his own muscles. He concentrated harder on the wall and the curtain, and their colors began to swirl and fade. Within seconds, they were gone, and the bug-filled passage seemed to continue on.

He knew he didn't have much time. As he stepped away from the wall, he opened his right pocket, returning the chameleons on his body to the Portal Place and stripping his camouflage. Then he charged down the hall about thirty steps, turned, and deliberately dropped to the floor, hoping to give the appearance that he'd fallen. He did his best to ignore the bugs crawling over him and stayed focused on what he needed to do.

DeGraff appeared from a hidden passage, his long, open trench coat flapping like a sheet hung out to dry. He was running faster than ever, which meant the Chamber of Lights hadn't caused him serious harm. Noah clambered to his feet, pretended to slip to his knees, then rose again. Once DeGraff was only a few steps away, Noah charged forward.

Panic rushed through him as he suddenly worried he might miss the curtain and crash into the wall. He kept to the middle of the corridor.

When he glanced back and saw little more than a black glove with outstretched fingers, he lowered his head and ran faster than he ever had in his life. Then, just as DeGraff grabbed his shirt, the curtains swept across Noah's body, sparking his nerves with their magic. Together, Noah and the Shadowist portaled into the City of Species.

He wrestled out of the clutches of DeGraff and fell into the arms of a teenage boy with thick sideburns and a jumble of spikes on his shoulders. People and animals were crowded around, and they jumped when they saw DeGraff. Several lions pulled back their heads and roared, and snakes slithered all about.

DeGraff had fallen and now lay on the ground, his arms drawn up to his face to protect it from the bright sunlight. He was moaning and writhing, his black boots marking the street.

Three Descenders moved in to apprehend him: a woman with a long tail; a teenage boy with dozens of small suction cups on his hands; and a woman with extra legs and hooked arms, like those of a praying mantis.

"Wait!" a familiar voice called out, and Noah turned to see Mr. Darby pushing through the crowd. Noah saw what Mr. Darby did: the sun was at the Descenders' backs, and their shadows were stretched out in front of them, sliding across the street toward DeGraff.

The Shadowist faced the Descenders and suddenly became still. Realizing his intentions, Noah jumped forward.

"Stop!" Mr. Darby commanded.

The Descenders did, but it was too late; their shadows had already fallen across DeGraff and onto the portal behind him.

For a second, DeGraff smiled. Then he was gone— through their shadows and back into the Secret Creepy Critters.

"Get him!" Mr. Darby commanded. *"Go!"*

As the Descenders charged, the curtains fell from the rod and were swept into the building, which immediately closed on the vacant spot, stone bricks appearing from nowhere. The gold curtain rings bounced and clattered and rolled through the Descenders' legs to rest in the street.

Mr. Darby pushed through the crowd and slammed his fists against the place the portal had been. He set the top of his head against the bricks and stayed that way, his long beard dangling. His sunglasses slipped an inch or two down his nose and then dropped off altogether, landing by his feet.

Noah simply stood there and watched. The City of Species fell silent—not a person spoke, not a bird chirped. The Descenders were deathly still. DeGraff had come to the Secret Society like a gift, and they'd failed to take him.

After some time, Mr. Darby drew back his head, tipped up his chin, and sucked in a deep breath. At last, he turned, and as the scouts looked into his eyes, Noah felt his insides drop.

His eyes were clouded by a milky white. As the old man turned to look at something, neither eye followed his movement.

Mr. Darby looked like he was blind.

The old man bent over, retrieved his sunglasses, and set them on his face. He reached out, grabbed the jacket of a nearby Descender, and pushed him with more strength than Noah would have believed possible. The Descender fell, shredding his jeans as he slid across the street.

All at once, the other Descenders dropped, each to one knee, and bowed their heads, like servants before a king.

"Fools!" Mr. Darby hollered. "He was *right here*"—he thrust a finger toward the ground—"and you failed to apprehend him!"

He stepped away from the place the portal had been and moved through the crowd, his head slowly turning as he seemed to gaze at the kneeling Descenders.

"Mr. Darby," one of the Descenders said without lifting his face. "We didn't—"

"*QUIET!*" Mr. Darby turned to the Descender. "How is it that—"

"Sir." Another Descender spoke without daring to raise his eyes. "Tank, Sam, Tameron, Hannah—they're all safe. Let's not forget."

Noah held his breath, certain the interruption would lead Mr. Darby to lash out. Instead, the old man seemed to calm.

"Yes," he said after some time. His voice was more relaxed, as if he'd suddenly remembered who he was. "They are safe." He waited a few seconds, then turned and split the crowd. Before he walked off in a rush, he said, "If only for now."

❧ CHAPTER 47 ❧

GOOD-BYE, FOR NOW

Once Mr. Darby was gone, the Descenders rose to their feet and traded nervous whispers. A few stood around the place the portal had been, touching different parts of the wall.

"Guys!"

Noah turned to the voice, and his heart lifted when he saw his friends parting the crowd. Richie and Megan were riding Little Bighorn, and Solana and the four Specters from the other mission were walking beside Blizzard. The polar bear was limping, and he had blood-stained gauzes over his injuries from the school. He looked thinner and weaker, but very much alive.

Noah and Ella ran to them, and instead of slowing down, Noah crashed into Blizzard, as if trying to tackle him. The mighty bear didn't budge, and Noah's arms wrapped around his thick, long neck. Noah's heart was racing, and something other than blood was rushing through his body, warming his legs, his arms, his fingers. He felt his eyes water, and he blinked away his tears before the Descenders could notice.

He pulled back his head for a good look at Blizzard and said, "I thought . . . I thought for sure I'd never see you again."

Blizzard curled up one side of his mouth and softly growled.

"I . . ." But Noah didn't know what to say, so instead he hugged Blizzard tight. Out of nowhere, he remembered himself as a small child, five years old perhaps. He saw himself standing in the underwater tunnel of the Polar Pool in the Clarksville Zoo, watching Blizzard swim just a few feet in front from him. At one point, the bear had set the pads of his meaty paws against the tunnel, and Noah had reached up and pressed his palms to the glass, so that nothing but a few inches separated them. At the time, Noah thought it would have been impossible to get closer to the mighty polar bear who lived just beyond his own backyard.

How wrong he had been.

Noah saw Ella hugging Little Bighorn, who had his neck curled around her, as if hugging her back. Richie was smiling and patting the rhino's side. Marlo flew down and took his usual perch on Noah's shoulder.

"I haven't forgotten about you," Noah said. "Nice work in there."

Marlo chirped. Then he ruffled his wings and flew off again. Noah watched him go, the small kingfisher who had started this impossible adventure more than a year ago by tapping on Noah's window late one night.

Blizzard turned his head and licked Noah's face, his enormous tongue nearly sweeping off Noah's cap. Noah smiled and wiped away the wetness. Then he glanced at Megan and Richie, saying, "Did you have problems?"

"Nothing like yours, apparently," Richie said. "DeGraff—you almost had him!"

Noah looked back at the place the portal had been. People were still standing around, rubbing their temples and shaking their heads. Two Descenders were having an argument, each blaming the other for what had happened.

"But we got our friends," Noah said. "And that's what we went in there to do."

"That's what *Evie* went in there to do," Jordynn said, and Noah looked to see her frowning. "When things settle down, you can bet Darby's going to want to talk to you guys about what you did today."

Noah nodded. He already knew the kind of trouble he might face.

"I got your back," Lee-Lee said. "Richie saved my butt out there—I'll make sure Darby and everyone else knows about that."

When everyone looked at Richie, he blushed and looked away. Ella held her fist up toward Richie, who awkwardly bumped his knuckles against hers.

"Where are they?" Noah asked. "Sam and Tank—those guys."

"There," Sara said. She was pointing to a big wooden wagon attached to an elephant. Near it, Tameron was being loaded onto a stretcher by three men in white suits—emergency workers, Noah guessed. Sam and Tank stood near their friend, and Hannah was holding his hand.

Megan and Richie slipped off Little Bighorn and the scouts quickly squeezed through the crowd and gathered around Tameron, who turned toward them and managed a slight smile. Ella hoisted Tameron's backpack with both hands, saying, "Your pack—we got it."

Tameron raised his free hand a few inches toward Ella, who nervously took it. The teenager tried to say something, realized he couldn't, and instead squeezed her fingers. Then he let his hand drop to his chest.

Ella gave the pack to Hannah to hold for Tameron.

The scouts moved aside for the emergency workers to hoist the stretcher, walk up a ramp, and secure the stretcher to the wagon. Hannah climbed aboard and kneeled beside her friend, again taking his hand. After a few seconds, the elephant trumpeted and the wagon pulled away.

Noah realized for the first time how terrible Sam and Tank looked—dark, glassy eyes and sunken faces. He took a step toward them and said, "Guys—you okay?"

Sam simply nodded, as if too exhausted for unnecessary words.

"Tameron . . ." Noah said with a glance toward the wagon. "Will he . . . will he be all right?"

"I think so."

As Sam suddenly lost his balance, Noah took a spot at his side and pulled the teenager's arm over his shoulder. "C'mon," he said as he took a step toward another elephant-drawn wagon. "Let's get you to a doctor."

He led Sam up the ramp and then helped him into a seat. As he turned to walk off, Sam stopped him, saying, "Kid . . ."

Noah turned. "Yeah?"

Sam held his fist toward Noah, who bumped his knuckles against it.

Noah felt a rush of pride. He tried to say something, but couldn't gather the words. Instead, he just nodded and then headed down the ramp, where a scrawny-looking Tank was making his way up.

"You look . . ." Noah's voice trailed off as he searched for something other than the truth, which came out anyway. "*Horrible.*"

Tank managed a joke: "Nothing a plate of cheeseburgers and a bucket of fries can't fix. I'll be okay," he added, more seriously. "Thanks, my man."

Once Noah was back on the ground, one of the emergency workers motioned for Blizzard to come aboard. As he walked past, Noah hugged him a final time. Then the bear settled into a spot near Sam. The worker lifted the ramp, boarded the elephant, and sent the wagon off.

As the scouts stood watching them go, Little Bighorn trotted up to them. Marlo swooped down again and perched on the tip of the rhino's horn.

Solana stepped over, touched Noah's shoulder, and mouthed, *Thanks.*

"Where's Evie?" Ella suddenly asked. "And what about Elakshi?"

"Hospital, already. And Evie's gone," Solana said. "The last place she wants to be is with a bunch of Descenders."

Noah thought to ask why, then decided against it. Right now, all he really wanted was to go home.

As the scouts headed out across the City of Species, they waved good-bye to Solana, Noah feeling less triumphant than he had after previous adventures. He started thinking about Mr. Darby—his unexpected anger, his strange eyes, the way the Descenders had bowed to him.

As the four friends hurried toward a portal that would take them home, Ella said, "We're out of here."

And in Noah's head, Mr. Darby's voice echoed: "If only for now."